Henry Cecil was the pseudony... ...... Leon. He was born in Norwo... London, England in 1902. He .... where he edited an undergraduate magazine and wrote a Footlights May Week production. Called to the bar in 1923, he served with the British Army during the Second World War. While in the Middle East with his battalion he used to entertain the troops with a serial story each evening. This formed the basis of his first book, *Full Circle*. He was appointed a County Court Judge in 1949 and held that position until 1967. The law and the circumstances which surround it were the source of his many novels, plays, and short stories. His books are works of great comic genius with unpredictable twists of plot which highlight the often absurd workings of the English legal system. He died in 1976.

ACCORDING TO THE EVIDENCE
ALIBI FOR A JUDGE
THE ASKING PRICE
BRIEF TALES FROM THE BENCH
BROTHERS IN LAW
THE BUTTERCUP SPELL
CROSS PURPOSES
DAUGHTERS IN LAW
FATHERS IN LAW
FRIENDS AT COURT
FULL CIRCLE
HUNT THE SLIPPER
INDEPENDENT WITNESS
MUCH IN EVIDENCE
NATURAL CAUSES
NO BAIL FOR THE JUDGE
NO FEAR OR FAVOUR
THE PAINSWICK LINE
PORTRAIT OF A JUDGE
SETTLED OUT OF COURT
SOBER AS A JUDGE
TELL YOU WHAT I'LL DO
UNLAWFUL OCCASIONS
THE WANTED MAN
WAYS AND MEANS
A WOMAN NAMED ANNE

TRUTH WITH HER BOOTS ON

by

Henry Cecil

HOUSE OF
STRATUS

This edition published in 2000 by House of Stratus, an imprint of Stratus Holdings plc, 24c Old Burlington Street, London, W1X 1RL, UK.

www.houseofstratus.com

Typeset, printed and bound by House of Stratus.

A catalogue record for this book is available from the British Library.

ISBN 1-84232-066-1

Contents

A lie travels round the world while truth is putting on her boots.

C H SPURGEON: *Truth and Falsehood*

CHAPTER ONE

To Help a Friend

Counsel for the accused was addressing the judge, his Honour Judge Whitehill, in mitigation of the offence of which his client had been found guilty.

'Your Honour,' he said, 'can any of us put our hands on our hearts and say that we would not have done what the accused did?'

This was not quite a rhetorical question, for counsel looked round the court at members of the Bar and solicitors, and eventually his eyes came to rest on those of the judge. He did not say, 'And that includes you, your Honour', but he meant it, and it was plain to the judge that he meant it too. Counsel's client had been found guilty of the offence of 'without reasonable excuse' assisting his wife to evade arrest in respect of an offence of which he knew or believed her to have been guilty. Counsel had endeavoured to persuade the jury that it was a reasonable excuse for a husband to help his wife in these circumstances simply because he was her husband, but the judge had flatly told the jury that, if they so decided, it would be a mistake in law.

'If I am wrong about that,' the judge had said, 'the Court of Appeal can put me right. What no doubt Parliament had in mind when it referred to "reasonable excuse" is, for

1

example, a case where the person who helped the criminal to evade arrest was under some form of duress or was deceived into giving assistance. It is, of course, quite natural for a husband to wish to protect his wife or a parent his child, but I do not believe that Parliament intended to license the members of a family to help one of them to evade arrest when they knew he or she had committed a crime.'

'Your Honour would not accept my submission,' went on counsel, 'on the issue of guilt, that ties of blood and affection are sufficient to give a person a reasonable excuse for helping the object of his affections. Naturally in this court I accept your Honour's ruling on that matter and quite frankly I think your Honour is probably right.'

'A comforting thought,' said the judge. 'Thank you.'

'But when it comes to a matter of sentence I feel on much firmer ground. Your Honour yourself said that it was natural for a husband to want to help his wife. But I venture to put it even higher than that. I would respectfully submit that a husband has a moral duty to assist his wife. Of course that cannot wipe out his legal duty, but in my respectful submission it should make a great difference when it comes to passing sentence.'

'I've got that point,' said the judge. 'Have you got any other?'

'I'm sure your Honour will take fully into consideration the fact that this is a first offence on the part of my client.'

'But not unfortunately,' said the judge, 'on the part of his wife.'

'That is perfectly true,' said counsel, 'but I hope your Honour will accept that my client has never sought to profit from his wife's misdemeanours. Your Honour will remember that the chief-inspector was very fair on that matter and said that he was quite satisfied that my client had tried to persuade his wife to give up shoplifting, that he had more than once returned anonymously goods which she had taken and that the only reason why he helped her to evade arrest was because of his affection for her and not because he wanted to share in the loot.'

'I accept all that,' said the judge.

'Then, in those circumstances,' said counsel, 'I hope your Honour will feel able to take a lenient course in the matter,' and he sat down.

'Leonard Newton,' said the judge, 'your learned counsel has asked me to take a lenient course with you. I should like to be able to do this, but I'm afraid I cannot. Nevertheless I agree with much of what your learned counsel has said. I personally would not think less of anyone who risked his liberty in defence of his wife or child. Indeed, such conduct is often to be admired. But the State cannot sanction it. It cannot give the green light to people who help criminals to avoid the consequences of their criminal acts. Nor, unfortunately, can I. I would not dissent from the proposition that a man may have a greater duty towards his wife or child than he has to the State. Certainly in cases other than treason and the like. But the duty to the State is a legal duty which its judges must enforce. The duty to wife or child is only a moral duty. A loving husband may well say to himself, "I will do anything for my wife and I will risk going to prison for her." But it must be made clear to husbands and parents and, I may add, very close friends that that is exactly what he will risk. If I were to pass a nominal sentence in this case I should in effect be licensing the concealment of crime by the close relatives of the criminal. We live in an age when there is too much lawlessness anyway and in my opinion it would be very wrong of me, however much I may sympathise with and even admire the conduct of the accused, to do anything to encourage such behaviour. It must be made known that, if a man does anything to assist his wife to avoid the consequences of her criminal acts, he will in all probability be sent to prison if found out. And I should make it plain too that in my view the same consequences should often apply to a woman who assists her husband. Of course different considerations will arise in cases where the wife is under the domination of her husband. Similarly, if a husband were under the domination of his wife, that circumstance might justify a more lenient sentence. But that is not the case here. The accused is a decent man with a profound affection for his wife and he has had a great deal to put up with in the past. She is becoming a confirmed shoplifter. I accept unreservedly that her husband has endeavoured to stop her and that he has never knowingly benefited from her crimes. It is an odd thing to say to a man who is going to be sent to prison what I am about to say to him. But I do say with a full appreciation of the words which I am using that the accused will leave the court without a stain on his moral character. I very much hope that, when he comes out of prison, no friend of his and no prospective employer will look upon him as a criminal or will think any the less of him for what he has done. And I hope that any employer to whom he may offer his services, if he has the necessary qualifications for the job, will consider him favourably for it, unless, somewhat inadvisedly, he should apply for a position in one of the multiple stores where his wife does her shopping. The sentence of the court is that you go to prison for twelve months.'

Judge Julian Whitehill lived alone with his wife Margaret in a comfortable house on the outskirts of London. He was very happily married and devoted to his wife, and he certainly had it in mind when he sentenced Leonard Newton that he would have done the same for his wife as Leonard Newton had done for his, although the chance of Margaret committing a serious crime was not one which was in the realms of possibility. He did realise that it is easy to say what you would do in given circumstances if you know perfectly well that those circumstances will never arise.

He had been a judge for fourteen years and would become entitled to retire on full pension in a year's time. But he had no intention of doing so. From a very early age he had been passionately interested in the truth. He was ten when he was told of the story of Cassandra, the Trojan prophetess who was cursed with what he thought was one of the most terrible curses which could be imposed on anyone, that she should always prophesy the truth and never be believed. The frustration engendered by this thought kept him awake for much of the night after he had been told the story.

The obvious profession for him was the Bar, where his ability to spot the weaknesses in his own clients' case and often to save them tremendous sums in costs by showing that they were in the wrong, rightly earned him a very large practice within a comparatively short time of his being called. He cross-examined his clients politely but very thoroughly in his own chambers at a very early stage in the proceedings or proposed proceedings. Sometimes his cross-examination was so thorough that clients were prompted to ask him on which side he was appearing. His solicitor would then point out that it was very much better for the proposed plaintiff to be cross-examined in a friendly way by his own counsel than to be shown to be a liar in court by a hostile cross-examining counsel. Able solicitors soon realised the value of employing Whitehill and learned to bring their problems to him at a very early stage. Often before proceedings were started at all. He was very rarely wrong in his assessment of a case. And the amount of money which he must have saved his clients in costs over the years was very considerable indeed. Although this often meant that lawyers made little out of a case, when, if it had been fought, they would have made hundreds or even thousands, curiously enough, contrary to what many members of the public think, a normal lawyer, whether counsel or solicitor, always prefers to advise settlement of a difficult case than to let his client take the risk of an expensive defeat. Fortunately for lawyers there are people who say and mean – at any rate at the time of saying it – that they don't care what a case costs them and are determined to bring it to court. Actually the expression they usually use is that they are determined to get justice. And when they are told – somewhat to their surprise – that bringing a case to court does not necessarily mean that they will get justice, they are in the first instance horrified. Many people think that, if you are in the right, you are bound to win. But this is not so. Judges are only human and they make mistakes. Witnesses who are most convincing in the witness box and who appear to be telling the truth may in fact be arrant liars and the judge may not see through them. Of course, if there were perfect justice, the man who was in the right would always win. But in such a state of affairs there would be no need for any law courts. Everyone would behave perfectly.

Judge Whitehill had another quality which made him a good judge. He did not worry over his cases after they were over. He took great trouble to try to get the answer right but, having given it, he turned his mind to other matters and, unless the case had some unusual quality, as often as not he forgot all about it. On the way home from sentencing Leonard Newton he did indeed let his mind dwell for a short time on the oddity of sending a man to prison with no stain on his character. But he did not wonder how Leonard Newton would get on in prison, how his wife would manage without him while he was there, whether she would get into trouble during that period, and how they would manage when he came out of prison. Certainly he hoped that things would go as well as possible for them, but he did not in the least brood upon their misfortunes.

However, when he got home he thought that the apparent anomaly of what he had said in sentencing the man would be of sufficient interest to tell his wife, but before he could do so, she said, 'Dick telephoned. He wants to see you rather urgently. I told him to come for coffee. Is that all right?'

'Why not dinner?'

'Hadn't enough and I simply hadn't time to go out and get another steak. Anyway it seems that he wanted to see you and not me. He sounded rather anxious as a matter of fact.'

'Daphne's not ill or anything like that?'

'Oh no. They're perfectly well. It's simply something he wants to see you about. It seems to be preying on his mind rather.'

'It will be nice to have a chat anyway.'

Richard Wetherall was the judge's oldest friend. They had been at school and Cambridge together and they knew as much about each other as two human beings, other than husband and wife, can know. Their trust in each other was absolute. It was pretty well impossible to think of either of them committing a serious crime, but had the impossible happened, the one could have

7

confessed it to the other with confidence that the burden of knowing about it would be cheerfully accepted and that there would be no possible risk of disclosure. It is perhaps not uninteresting for the average person to consider how many of his friends fall into that class. There are plenty of peccadilloes which otherwise respectable people commit and sometimes they are inclined to boast about them to their friends and even to their acquaintances. Cheating the Customs and the Revenue is looked upon by many people as no worse than a motoring offence. Not so shoplifting or murder. But there is a considerable difference between these last two. How many friends has the average person to whom he could safely confess to murder? Few friends, if any, would consider it their duty to inform the police that a person had admitted to shoplifting, but quite a number would feel that murder was a different matter and had to be disclosed. But apart from the fear of disclosure, which would limit the number to whom you could safely confess, there would also be reluctance, in the case of an old and valued friend, to impose the burden on him of knowing of the crime without feeling able to notify the authorities about it. You may trust your friend not to give you away, but you may feel that it is not fair to embarrass him by your confession. If a really reliable opinion poll were taken on the subject it would be interesting to know how many friends of this calibre the average person has.

Richard Wetherall had become an accountant when his friend Julian Whitehill went to the Bar. Richard had done extremely well, was happily married, with three children, and could certainly be described as·one of the lucky people in the world. As far as one could tell, he had no serious financial, business or domestic worries. To a large extent good luck of this kind comes from within. There are plenty of apparently happy and successful people with no grave problems to worry about, who worry the whole time. And there are plenty of people who are nothing like so lucky in their financial, business and domestic affairs who are usually happy in spite of the problems with which they have to deal. This is not in the least to say they are happy-go-lucky or pretend not to see the difficulties around them. They see them clearly enough and they deal with them to the best of their ability. But their nature is such that they are cheerful and happy most of the time, whatever problems they have to face. Both the judge and his friend were very similar in this respect. In consequence they both led happy lives.

But that evening Dick disclosed to the judge that he had a problem which he was hoping to solve in a way which, he did not realise, would create a very much greater problem for the judge. Dick, though happily married, had on one occasion some ten years before his visit to the judge gone to bed with another woman. His wife was unaware of this, but must have had some instinctive feeling about it. As a consequence her jealousy, which had always been rather above average, became rather too much for Dick's comfort. In spite of this, some time later, during his wife's absence for a few days, he had taken a young woman acquaintance out to lunch. That was all there was to it. On her return he told his wife. Whether or not it was due to her intuition about the episode ten years previously, his wife was extremely unpleasant about the innocent luncheon date. She cross-examined him about it and threatened to leave him if he did it again. She quite frightened Dick, who was horrified at the idea of his home being broken up. But his consciousness of guilt in respect of the ten-year-old episode did a great deal to counteract his feelings of innocence about the innocuous lunch. So he made up his mind there and then, not that he would never take another woman out to lunch in his wife's absence, but that he would make certain that his wife never learned about it.

Shortly before Dick's visit to the judge Daphne Wetherall had gone away for a day or two, and once again Dick had consoled himself for her absence by taking an attractive woman friend out to dinner. There was nothing more to it than that and he had been careful to go to a restaurant where they were not likely to meet anybody who knew them. Nevertheless when his wife returned she started to cross-examine him.

'Where did you dine on Friday?' she asked. For a moment he considered telling the truth, but then, fearing for the consequences of doing this, he decided to lie and lie quickly. The split second which he had wasted in considering whether to tell the truth was such a long one that his wife had time to say, 'Well?' before he could answer. He realised then that the lie would have to be a good one.

'I was with Julian at the club.'

'Sure?' asked his wife.

'Of course I'm sure. Why are you so suspicious?'

'I just like to know,' said Daphne. She paused and then added, 'The truth is, of course, that I'm as jealous as a cat where you're concerned. And, apart from that, it doesn't do a wife any good for other people to see her husband lunching or dining with attractive women. It makes a fool of her.'

'I take it,' said Dick, 'that my dining with Julian doesn't make a fool of you.'

'Don't be silly. *If* you did.'

'Ask him,' said Dick. 'If I were you I shouldn't appear to be too curious or that would make a fool of you too.'

'I'm not going to ring him up straight away, if that's what you mean,' said Daphne. 'But I'll bring up the subject somehow when we next meet.'

'You really are extraordinary,' said Dick. 'Why don't you believe me?'

'I do, as a matter of fact,' said Daphne. 'If you'd said you'd dined with anybody else I might still have been suspicious. But there's one person in the world who wouldn't lie to me. That's Julian. He wouldn't lie to anyone. Truth is pretty well his God. Unfortunately for some people who appear in front of him.'

After this conversation Dick lost little time in going to see the judge. Margaret brought them coffee in the judge's study and left them alone. They talked about other matters for a short time and then Dick raised the subject.

'I'm sorry to have to worry you with this,' he said, 'but it's rather awkward. I've made an ass of myself and brought you into it. I'm terribly sorry.'

He then explained what had happened. The judge listened without comment until he'd finished. Then: 'Why on earth did you have to do it?' he asked.

'You mean take the girl out to dinner?'

'No, of course not. Lie about it.'

Dick explained what had happened the time before.

'Daphne's grossly unreasonable,' said the judge.

'She is and she isn't,' said Dick. 'On the face of it she is, but the truth is that ten years ago I did have a one-night affair, although she knew and knows absolutely nothing about it. I suppose a woman's instincts are a form of extra-sensory perception.'

'It doesn't only happen with women,' said the judge. 'A man may have got away with several thefts and then be run in for one which he didn't do. The police have a feeling that he did the others but they can't prove it. Very

11

occasionally indeed they frame him and on other occasions, if there is some evidence against him, they improve it a bit. It's extraordinary how indignant a man becomes if he's unjustly convicted of a crime when he's committed plenty of others for which he has not even been prosecuted. Well, what d'you want me to do?'

'Nothing, if Daphne never asks you.'

'But if she does, you want me to corroborate you.'

'I know it's a dreadful thing to ask, but I can't see what else I can do. If Daphne found out I was telling lies she'd fear the worst – and, although there'd be no justification whatever for her suspicions, I really believe she'd leave me.'

'You mean,' said the judge, 'that she'd ask herself why you should have lied unless there was something more to it.'

'Exactly. And the trouble is that there is something more to it, although it happened ten years ago.'

'The same woman?'

'Oh no.'

'That's something,' said the judge, 'but it still leaves me with my problem.'

Daphne was quite right in thinking that the judge was a truthful person. There was nothing particularly odd in that. All Her Majesty's judges invariably tell the truth in public and almost invariably in private. That is not to say that some of them don't tell lies for other people's benefit. Ordinary social lies are told by almost everyone. One cannot even imagine an Archbishop, on being asked if he liked the soup, saying that it was undrinkable (as indeed it was). How many people of integrity who have seen a play by an author who is a friend of theirs and have been asked by him how they liked it have not, when necessary, lied? Some people pretend that such statements are not lies. They call them white lies or social lies or something of that kind. But they are in fact lies, that is deliberate misstatements of fact or opinion which are intended to deceive. Sometimes it would be unkind, sometimes rude and sometimes absolutely wrong not to tell them.

Unfortunately for the judge, however, the lie which he was being asked to tell did not come into this category at all. One of the reasons for the high reputation which English judges have is the complete trust which most people put in their integrity. One cannot imagine for a moment a judge evading the truth in order to get out of the consequences of a motoring offence. Many judges (perhaps not quite all) observe the speed limit, considering that it would not look well for a judge to be convicted even of that comparatively venial offence. And they realise that there is only one way to ensure that they are never convicted and that is by not breaking the law. The only way to get a reputation for telling the truth is always to tell it. If you lie to only one person that person may eventually learn that you have done so.

'I wouldn't have asked you if I could possibly have avoided it, but, having committed myself, I couldn't see what else I could do. I'm terribly sorry.'

'Perhaps,' said the judge, not very hopefully, 'the occasion won't arise.'

'I'm afraid it will,' said Dick.

'Well, you can count on me,' said the judge, 'but I must admit that I wish you'd come to borrow ten thousand pounds, which I may add I would have had great difficulty in lending to you.'

CHAPTER TWO

The Penalty

Within a week the occasion had arisen and the judge had confirmed Dick's story. Daphne believed him implicitly and was very much relieved. Dick, too, was very much relieved. The only person who was very far from relieved was the judge.

Dick and Daphne and Julian and Margaret had been dining together. On the way home Julian decided that he must tell his wife what he had done and what the consequences of it must be.

'I'm very cross with myself,' he began, 'but really I don't know what else I could do.'

'What *are* you talking about, Julian darling?'

'I'm going to have to resign,' he said.

'What on earth d'you mean? Only a couple of months ago you said that you weren't going to give up until you had to and you've got another seven or eight years. Good Lord, are you ill or something?'

'No, I'm perfectly well. But I shall have to do it. It's a bloody nuisance, but I can't see any alternative.'

Julian then told Margaret what had happened.

'But why on earth should you resign?' she asked. 'You're the only person who's done nothing wrong. Daphne's ridiculously jealous. Dick was ridiculously frightened and

14

told a thumping lie and all you do is to keep their marriage going for them. What's it got to do with being a judge anyway?'

'That's what most lay people would say,' said the judge, 'and I suppose some of my colleagues would say the same, though I hope not. I have told a blatant lie to a friend who trusted me completely. The reason that judges are so trustworthy in this country is because they don't do that sort of thing. Daphne knew that, if I backed up her husband, it was because he must have been telling the truth. I'm not being emotional or sentimental on the subject and you can say I'm being priggish if you like, but I've betrayed that trust. Having done so, I can't still remain on the Bench. How can I judge people after that? How can I say that I don't believe Mr X or that Mr Y has tried to deceive me? If I'm trying a divorce case how can I deal with counsel's submissions that it's a serious thing for a man to lie to his wife or something of that kind when I've been a party to it myself? And carry the matter a bit further. I hope that Dick and Daphne's marriage will last, but with somebody as jealous as she is, something of the sort might happen again and there might be proceedings and I might be called as a witness. Then I would have to admit that I had told a thumping lie. It's not merely that it would look bad for me. It would look bad for the whole Bench. People don't believe that judges can do such things. And I shouldn't have, if I could possibly have avoided it. I had to make a choice and naturally I didn't tell Dick or he wouldn't have let me.'

'But it's entirely a private matter,' said Margaret.

'It is at the moment,' said Julian, 'and probably will remain so, but first of all that isn't absolutely certain and secondly I take the view that, if a judge does something that no judge ought to do, he must resign. I think I was right to do it or I wouldn't have done it. Oddly enough a little while ago I had rather a similar case.'

'Not another judge?' asked Margaret.

'Oh good Lord no. No, it was the case of a man who protected his wife, who was a shoplifter, and I sent him to prison for twelve months and said he left the court without a stain on his character.'

'Can't you consult somebody about it?' asked Margaret. 'It really does seem too absurd, and it's too priggish for words, as you admit yourself.' Then another thought struck her. 'Won't it affect your pension?'

'Unfortunately,' said Julian, 'that's perfectly true. I shan't get a pension at all. I had wondered whether I could hang on for another year in order to get it, but it's absolutely impossible to do so in my view. I must never sit again. What the hell I shall do is another matter.'

In coming to his decision Julian had not even considered what would happen to him after resignation. But there was going to be a very serious problem for a man who had devoted most of his life to a search for the truth suddenly to be deprived of the opportunity of searching for it.

'Fortunately,' he went on, 'I had that huge case in the year before I became a judge. In those days the tax man let you keep it. So with what you've got we shall still be comfortably off.'

'But you've earned your pension,' said Margaret. 'Most of it anyway. Why can't you have a part of it?'

'Because you can't,' said Julian. 'If you retire on the ground of ill-health, yes, they'll let you have a part of it then. But if you resign before you've done fifteen years for your own private reasons then you get nothing at all. Of course I'll get the old age pension in due course, because I shan't be earning anything else.'

'What reason will you give for resigning?'

'I shan't. I suppose I shall have to say it's for personal reasons and so I'd better add that we're very happy, otherwise people will imagine that it's something of that kind.'

'Well, I shall speak to Dick,' said Margaret. 'He won't let you resign.'

'He can't stop me. He wouldn't have let me back him up if he'd known what the consequences would be.'

'But he'll feel awful.'

'He'll have to get over it. After all, I shall have to.'

'And what about me?'

'So you can't bear the thought of having to see so much more of me.'

'I can't bear the thought of your being treated so unfairly. You've been a splendid judge for fourteen years and you deserve a good pension.'

'What's money? Provided you have enough of it to live in reasonable comfort, who can want more?'

'I shall have to find you something to do,' said Margaret.

'That is a problem, I agree. I think I shall investigate some of the doubtful old cases.'

'A bit late for the people concerned. What you enjoy is investigating current problems.'

'That's true. But how am I going to do that now?'

'Why not go and speak to the Lord Chief about it? You know him quite well and he's a very understanding person.'

'This is a matter on which I've got to make my own decision. I think it's possible that he'd say that what I'd done was nothing to do with my judicial life and that it was quite unnecessary for me to resign.'

'What would he have done himself?'

'I don't think he would have lied.'

17

'Well, if he should say you could carry on, why isn't that right?' asked Margaret.

'Because I think that a judge is in the unique position that, as far as his personal behaviour is concerned, he cannot distinguish between his judicial and his private life. We all know about the judge in the last century who was found dead in a brothel. That was such a horrifying thing that even the Press hushed it up and they simply reported that he'd been found dead in a particular house and his body brought back to the judges' lodgings.'

'That was quite a different thing,' said Margaret.

'Of course it was,' said Julian. 'Every case is different. But in my view when you accept appointment to the Bench you accept the obligation never to do anything in any circumstances of which a man could be seriously ashamed.'

'Wait a moment,' said Margaret. 'You're not ashamed of what you did for Dick. You did it because you thought it was right and you thought your duty to your old friend was greater than your duty to Daphne or to the State.'

'That's perfectly true,' said Julian. 'No, I'm not ashamed. I'll have to amend that proposition. He must never do anything that a reasonable person might seriously disapprove of. And in my case, in fact, it's rather worse. When you come to think of it, it could well be said that I was guilty of a crime.'

'A crime!'

'Yes. Of conspiracy. Dick and I put our heads together to deceive Daphne into thinking that she had no case for alleging that the marriage had broken down. It's certainly arguable that that was a criminal conspiracy.'

'But you didn't put your heads together at all,' said Margaret. 'Dick came along and asked you to do it for him and you reluctantly agreed.'

'In exactly the same way,' said Julian, 'as a man about to commit a burglary seeks help from his friend, who reluctantly agrees. In such a case all I can say is that the friend must reluctantly go to prison.'

'Well, I shall go and see the Lord Chief,' said Margaret.

'I'd rather you didn't.'

'Why shouldn't I?'

'Of course you can, but there are two reasons why I suggest that you shouldn't.'

'One good one will do,' said Margaret.

'The best reason is that it won't make any difference.'

'What's the other reason?'

'If I'm going to resign, there's no particular reason why my conduct should be disclosed to other people.'

'One other person,' said Margaret. 'He wouldn't tell anyone else.'

'Of course he wouldn't. But he would know that I was a person who under given circumstances was prepared to tell a gross lie. I think I'm doing sufficient penance by resigning without making my fault known to one of the heads of the judiciary.'

'You're too good for this world,' said Margaret.

'Not in the least,' said Julian. 'I simply have a logical mind.'

'I bet there are other judges on the Bench who have told lies just as bad as yours.'

'Not since they became judges,' said Julian. 'Some of them may have lied to their wives. No doubt most of them have told the normal lies which we all tell to make life socially tolerable. But I doubt if any of them has conspired with a friend to deceive somebody else. Anyway, all I can say is that my mind is made up.'

'I wish Dick had said he'd been with me and then you wouldn't have been dragged into it at all.'

'Yes. That is rather a pity,' said Julian.

'Can't we pretend that that's what he really said?'

'We couldn't anyway because that would be just as bad. Rather worse even. But if it's any consolation to you, it's too late for that. I've already said that Dick was with me.'

'Well, at any rate,' said Margaret, 'we'll be able to take our holidays when we want them.'

'There'll be lots of advantages like that,' said Julian. 'If only I could find something to get my teeth into – something to keep my mind exercised, I should really rather enjoy it.'

'We must think something out,' said Margaret.

'I've already been trying.'

The next day Julian sent in his resignation and after the Lord Chancellor had recovered from his surprise another judge, Judge Rokeby, was appointed. The new judge asked Julian to come to court with him on his first day to introduce him to the officials and he willingly did so. On the way to the court Rokeby asked him whether he'd be prepared to sit on the Bench with him that morning and to give him an unbiased opinion of his behaviour.

'Certainly. I'd enjoy it.'

'I remember reading in some judge's reminiscences that he said he'd have been a much better judge in his first years if some experienced judge had given him a half-hour's talk before he started sitting. You can do that for me, if you will.'

'I'm sure it won't be at all necessary, but I'll be delighted to sit with you.'

CHAPTER THREE

An Accident Case

'Broad against Crane,' called the clerk and Mr Fergus, counsel for the plaintiff, rose.

'The facts,' he said, 'are quite simple, your Honour. The plaintiff is a young man of twenty-eight, living with his parents. He is a very keen amateur footballer. He lives in a small road called Shallow Place which goes off the main London road which your Honour will see on the plan in front of you. It was about six o'clock in the evening on the 19th November last when the plaintiff was going to post a letter. He walked along the pavement on the same side of the road as his house is and, when he was about two or three yards from the junction, there being no traffic coming out from or going down Shallow Place, he started to walk across the road. He had only taken one step into the road when the defendant, apparently wanting to go down Shallow Place from the London road, turned into it and ran over the plaintiff's toe. Then, apparently changing his mind, the driver turned back into the London road and went off without stopping. The lighting is not good there and it is quite possible that the defendant was unaware that he had had an accident. For that reason no criminal proceedings were taken against him for failing to stop after the accident. The plaintiff was able to take his number and, liability being denied on behalf of the defendant, the case comes before your Honour. So far as damages are concerned, the plaintiff's right big toe was broken and this has interfered with his playing football and is likely to do so for some considerable time. The agreed medical report puts the total period of incapacity for playing football at about a year. There is no special damage, so the only matters in respect of which your Honour is asked to award damages are the pain and suffering and, far more important, deprivation of a year's pleasure.'

The plaintiff Arthur Broad gave evidence in accordance with counsel's statement and it was only when the defendant's counsel, Mr Bowlby, started to cross-examine the witness that the somewhat unusual nature of the case emerged.

'Are you quite sure,' asked counsel, 'that the accident happened in Shallow Place and not in the main road?'

'Absolutely.'

'How far down Shallow Place did you say?'

'Not very far.'

'What do you mean by that? An inch or two, a foot or two, a yard or what?'

'A couple of yards or so, I should say.'

'But no doubt at all that it was in Shallow Place and not in the main road?'

'I've just said so.'

'So, according to your evidence, the defendant thought he wanted to go down Shallow Place, changed his mind and did a sort of arc of a circle and out of it again.'

'That's right.'

'You agreed that he might not have noticed that he ran over your toe owing to the street lighting?'

'Yes.'

'Surely he must have seen that you were there? There wasn't a fog. It wasn't pitch black. There simply wasn't much lighting there.'

'What is the question?' asked Judge Rokeby. 'Does the witness agree with all those statements of fact?'

'Yes,' said the plaintiff.

'You're quite a good-sized young man and, if the driver was keeping a reasonable look-out, surely he must have seen you.'

'Probably he saw me but he may not have noticed that my right foot was immediately in front of his wheel. It all happened in a flash.'

'Did you shout when you were struck?'

'No. For a moment I was too shocked and surprised.'

'Not too shocked and surprised to take his number?'

'Well, I took it.'

'But you didn't go to the police?'

'I didn't know my toe was broken until two or three days later when I went to the hospital because it was hurting so much.'

'What are you, Mr Broad?'

'I'm unemployed at the moment.'

'What were you doing at the time of the accident?'

'Going to post.'

'No, I mean what was your job at the time of the accident?'

'I was working in a bookmaker's office.'

'Is that your usual work?'

'I've had various jobs. I've no particular skills.'

'Except at football,' put in Judge Rokeby.

'That's right, your Honour.'

'Now I suggest to you,' said counsel for the defendant, 'that, if there was an accident at all, which my client disputes entirely, it must have taken place in the London road.'

'It didn't.'

'My client will tell his Honour that he never turned into Shallow Place, that he never had the slightest intention of turning into Shallow Place, that he has never been to Shallow Place in his life and that he didn't want to go to Shallow Place. That he had no business there and that he knew no one there and that he knew no one in the neighbourhood and that he was on his way home along the London road when all he had to do was to drive straight along about five miles beyond Shallow Place and then turn right at the large crossroads, which is a light-controlled crossing.'

'What is the question?' asked Judge Rokeby.

'I'm sorry, your Honour,' said counsel, 'perhaps I'd better put it this way. For the reasons which I have stated, I suggest to you that either you've made up this story of the accident or must have imagined it.'

'Well,' said Judge Rokeby, 'you're not disputing that he broke his toe, I presume, because there's an agreed medical report.'

'No, your Honour, we're not disputing that.'

'Are you suggesting to the witness that he has broken his toe in some other way?'

'Your Honour,' said counsel, 'I'll be quite frank about this. If the plaintiff had said that the accident took place in the London road, although my client categorically denies that anything of the sort took place, obviously it would be possible that at night a motorist might not notice that he had run over somebody's toe. It's unlikely but possible. If that had been the case, I should merely have suggested that he was mistaken. But my client says that this story of

his going in and out of Shallow Place is utterly untrue.
Now there can't be a mistake about that, your Honour.'

'Your client might have forgotten, I suppose,' said Judge
Rokeby.

'My client says that he has never been up Shallow Place
in his life and that there is no other turning near there
which he has been up. It is therefore in the highest degree
improbable that he could have made a mistake about this.
If my client has not made a mistake, he is either lying or
telling the truth. In my submission the same must apply
to the plaintiff and it is my duty to put the case to him on
that basis.'

'Well,' said Judge Rokeby to the witness, 'did you break
your toe in some other form of accident or as a result of its
being run over by the defendant's car?'

'It was the defendant's car.'

'Are you sure of that?'

'Absolutely, and I've a witness to prove it.'

'Never mind about the witness,' said counsel. 'Are you
quite sure that what you've told his Honour is the truth?'

'I'm on oath.'

'Everyone who gives evidence is on oath,' said counsel.
'Are you sure?'

'Why should I make up such a story?'

'You're not supposed to ask me questions,' said counsel,
'but as you have, I don't mind answering it. Admittedly
you broke your toe but it's perfectly possible to do that by
striking it at home, in the dark or in some way like that.
But no one would pay you any money for that.'

'This is a very serious matter,' said Judge Rokeby. 'The
suggestion to you, Mr Broad, is that, having broken your
toe in some ordinary accident, nothing whatever to do
with the defendant, you deliberately made up this story
about his running over your toe in order to get damages

out of him. In other words, that you have attempted to obtain money from him by fraud, that is to say by falsely pretending that you've injured your toe in an accident, when nothing of the kind had happened and you'd simply stubbed your toe, or something of that sort. It is alleged that you are committing perjury. Is there the slightest truth in any of this?'

'None at all, your Honour.'

'Yes, Mr Bowlby?' said Judge Rokeby. 'Any further questions?'

'No, your Honour.'

That concluded the evidence of the plaintiff, and the witness to whom he had referred when he gave his evidence was then called. He was a Mr Loudwater. In answer to the plaintiff's counsel he said that he lived in Putney, that he had never known the plaintiff or the defendant before the accident, and that he knew nobody in Shallow Place or indeed in that neighbourhood. That he had gone for a walk, that he was going down the London road and that, when he came to Shallow Place, for some reason that he couldn't really remember he decided to go down it. That he went to the end of it and then turned round. Just before he reached the London road he saw the plaintiff walking ahead of him, he saw him walk into the roadway and then he saw the defendant's car come into Shallow Place from the London road, run over the plaintiff's foot and then run out again into the London road and go off. He went up to the plaintiff to see if he had been hurt and, if so, how badly, and he gave him his name and address.

Defendant's counsel then got up to cross-examine.

'What is your job, Mr Loudwater?' he began.

'I'm with a security firm.'

'For how long have you had that job?'

'About eighteen months.'

'How old are you?'

'Thirty-three.'

'What were you doing before you went to the security firm?'

'I was unemployed for a time.'

'For how long?'

'About twelve months.'

'And then what did you do?'

'I was in a greengrocer's.'

'For how long were you there?'

'About six months.'

'And before that?'

'I was unemployed.'

'For how long?'

'For about two years.'

'And what were you doing before you were unemployed?'

'What's that got to do with it?'

'Just answer the question,' said the judge. 'Counsel is entitled to ask it.'

'But what's my private life got to do with the case?'

'I'll tell you,' said Judge Rokeby. 'Counsel may be going to suggest to you that you've invented or imagined this accident and, if he is, he is entitled to see what sort of a person you are.'

'He can see that,' said the witness, 'without asking all these questions.'

'You've seen me for about half an hour,' said counsel, following up the judge's line of approach, 'but you can't tell from that what sort of a man I am.'

'Oh, can't I?' said the witness. 'You ask too many bloody questions.'

'Don't talk like that,' said Judge Rokeby. 'If I think that counsel is asking questions which he shouldn't ask, I shall stop him.'

'In order to know what a man is like,' said counsel, 'you've got to know something about him. If he's married or single, what his home life is like, the jobs he's had and so forth. I've been asking you about your jobs. How many jobs have you had since you left school?'

'I wouldn't rightly know.'

'But a good number?'

'How many have you had?' asked the witness.

'You can't ask counsel questions,' said Judge Rokeby.

'That doesn't seem fair.'

'It's perfectly fair. Counsel is employed to investigate your claim and he's bound to do it by all proper means allowed by the law.'

'If I'd known this was going to happen,' said the witness, 'I wouldn't have given my name to Mr Broad.'

'Wouldn't you?' said counsel. 'Why did you give it?'

'Because I saw what happened.'

'But that wouldn't have been much use to the plaintiff if you hadn't been prepared to go to court to say it happened,' said counsel.

'Well, I've come.'

'I know you have, but you've just said that you wouldn't have come if you'd been told you were going to be asked these questions.'

'Well, I wouldn't have.'

'What did you think would happen when you came to court?'

'I've never been to court before, so I've no idea. I thought I'd just have to say what happened and then I could go home.'

28

'How could the learned judge say whether your story is true unless it was tested by my asking questions?'

'I don't know what you mean.'

'My client is going to say that no accident took place.'

'Then he's a liar.'

'What other jobs have you had except the ones you've mentioned?'

'I can't remember everything.'

'Have you had so many that you can't remember them?'

'I've got to think. Some of them I only held for a few months.'

'You've not been with a scrap-metal merchant, by any chance?'

'How did you know?'

Counsel for the plaintiff rose. 'What exactly did my learned friend imply by asking that question?'

'I wanted to know if he'd been employed by a scrap-metal merchant.'

'Did my learned friend intend to imply by that that my client's witness was not a person of good character?'

'I simply wanted to know if your client's witness had been employed by a scrap-metal merchant.'

'Yes,' said the judge, 'but why? There are a thousand jobs which the plaintiff might have had and, unless you have instructions that this witness was employed by a scrap-metal merchant, why did you mention it?'

'Well, your Honour,' said counsel, 'this is a serious case as I have already pointed out. I want to see how reliable this witness is. He seems to have been in and out of jobs all his life. People in the scrap-metal trade are not always reliable.'

'You mean,' said the judge, 'that some of them are convicted of crime and go to prison?'

'That's perfectly true,' said counsel.

'You're not suggesting that that's happened to this witness?'

'No,' said counsel. 'He's sworn that he's of good character and I accept that.'

'Then,' said the plaintiff's counsel, 'what on earth has the question got to do with the case?'

'It has not a great deal of relevance,' said counsel for the defendant, 'but it has a little. If a man is in and out of jobs and some of those jobs are in businesses where some of the people concerned are not reputable, that to a certain extent, your Honour, reflects on the witness' character.'

'Are you suggesting,' said the judge, 'that more than half of the people engaged in the scrap-metal trade are dishonest, irresponsible or unreliable?'

'I have no idea,' said counsel. 'I only know that the trade has a reputation for employing such people.'

'Are you suggesting that this witness is dishonest, irresponsible or unreliable?'

'In this case, yes, your Honour.'

'In his general character?'

Counsel thought for a moment. 'Yes, I suppose I am, your Honour. I'm going to suggest that having regard to this witness' past and his evidence in the witness box, that combining the two together he is not a person whose evidence your Honour should accept.'

'Any more questions?' asked the judge.

'After the accident did you go with the plaintiff back to his home?'

'Yes, I did,' said the witness. 'And he gave me a cup of tea. And,' added the witness, 'something else, if you want to know.'

'Well,' said counsel. 'What was it?'

'A piece of cake.'

'While you were having your tea and cake, did either of you suggest going to the police?'

'We didn't know that his toe had been broken.'

'But it had been run over.'

'Well, the driver might have said he hadn't seen him.'

'But you couldn't tell that until he'd been asked. You knew that there'd been an accident.'

'I've said so.'

'You knew the defendant hadn't stopped. If the defendant ran over the plaintiff's toe, surely he must have seen it.'

'He might have been thinking of something else.'

'But normally the driver would have seen him if he'd been keeping a proper look-out.'

'He wouldn't have run over his toe, if he had been.'

'Did you think that the driver had seen him?'

'He should have.'

'And you knew he hadn't stopped.'

'Of course I knew it.'

'Then here was a driver who, to your knowledge, had had an accident and who, to your knowledge, hadn't stopped. Why didn't you report that fact to the police?'

'It wasn't for me to report anything. For all I knew, Mr Broad did report it.'

'You know now that he didn't.'

'I've been told so.'

'Did you discuss reporting it when you had your tea and cake?'

'I'm not sure. We might have.'

'You mean you can't remember one way or the other whether you said to him or he said to you, "I think we'd better go to the police" or something of the sort?'

'We might have.'

'And you can't remember one way or the other whether you did or you did not?'

'No, I can't. I can't remember everything. I'm not a computer.'

After the defendant's counsel had finished his cross-examination of Mr Loudwater he called the defendant to give his version of the story.

The defendant, John Crane, said he was aged forty, married and lived in Chingford. He was a copywriter employed by a firm of advertising agents and had been so employed for the past twenty years. He said that he was driving home on the occasion in question along the London road. He did not turn down or half turn down any turning on the way along the London road and he had had no accident.

'Do you know Shallow Place?' asked his counsel.

'I do now,' said the defendant, 'but I didn't on the occasion in question. After the claim was made I drove down there and had a look at it. I have never walked down there or driven down there in my life. I know no one there or in the neighbourhood.'

'Have you ever driven down a similar turning in that neighbourhood, or half driven down it? That is to say, have you ever turned into it and out of it almost at once?'

'Never,' said the defendant.

'Have you ever been in court before in your life?'

'Never.'

'At the time of the accident were you insured against this type of accident?'

'Yes.'

'If your insurance company has to pay the plaintiff's claim, do you lose your no-claim bonus?'

'No, because I haven't got one. I have a policy which doesn't provide for no-claim bonuses. You can make as many claims as you like and your premium will be the same next year, except to the extent that it may have gone up in the ordinary way.'

'Have you ever in your life told a lie in order to avoid paying your just debts?'

'Never.'

'Have you ever told a lie in order to persuade somebody to pay something to you?'

'Never.'

The defendant's counsel sat down and the plaintiff's counsel rose to cross-examine.

'Mr Crane,' he began, 'do you agree that at the time the plaintiff says there was an accident involving his big toe you must have been somewhere in the neighbourhood of Shallow Place?'

'Yes, but I did not turn into it or half turn into it. I drove straight along the London road and never turned off anywhere.'

'You didn't drive in a straight line all the way?'

'How d'you mean?'

'I mean,' said counsel, 'that, like most drivers, while you were driving along the road, sometimes you veered a little to the right and sometimes to the left. I don't mean that you were zigzagging or anything of that sort. In the nature of things, either because of some hole in the road or because there was some obstruction, you would veer a little to the right or to the left.'

'Yes, of course.'

'And even when there wasn't any obstruction or hole in the road you didn't keep a geometrically straight course. You may have turned a little to the right or a little to the left for no particular reason.'

'I didn't make any sudden turn.'

'I'm not for the moment suggesting that you did anything improper, Mr Crane, but you've driven for a good many years, I take it?'

'About twenty.'

'And it must be your experience that, when you drive, sometimes inadvertently the car goes a little too near the kerb or a little too near the middle of the road and as and when necessary you correct it?'

'Yes, of course.'

'Now occasionally, possibly very occasionally, have you not found yourself going much too much to one side of the road or the other? I don't mean crossing on to the wrong side of the road or going on to the pavement but taking a course which would have resulted in that if you hadn't corrected it.'

'I suppose so.'

'I don't know whether you're one of the drivers who happen to notice attractive young women when you're driving?'

'I keep a good look-out, if that's what you mean.'

'For such attractive young women, do you mean?' asked the judge.

'Oh no, your Honour, though naturally I see them from time to time, and I must admit that occasionally I have looked at them rather too long. But not so long as to cause an accident or anything like it.'

'You had no business in Shallow Place?'

'None at all.'

'So that if by accident you had swerved into it you would have wanted to swerve out of it as quickly as possible?'

'This would have been very difficult, if not impossible, for me to do at the speed at which I was going.'

'How fast were you going?'

'About thirty miles an hour. If I'd wanted to turn into Shallow Place I would have had to slow down and then turn. I've tested it since and going at thirty miles an hour I think it would be pretty well impossible, except conceivably for a racing driver, to turn in and out of the road as it's said I did, without having a bad accident.'

'Exactly,' said counsel. 'You did have an accident. You ran over somebody's toe.'

'I did nothing of the kind.'

'Although I'm prepared to accept that normally you're a careful driver,' went on counsel, 'I assume that from time to time, apart altogether from attractive young women, you must have taken your eye off the road and given yourself a start.'

'I can't recollect any particular occasion.'

'I daresay you can't, but isn't it a thing that happens to every driver? Some more than others. To all of us at least very occasionally.'

'I expect so.'

'I suggest to you that that's what happened on this occasion and that for one reason or another, as you reached Shallow Place, possibly your speed had decreased owing to traffic in front of you and you swerved into Shallow Place, not very much, and swerved out again.'

'If that had happened I should have remembered it. Nothing of the sort happened. Nothing of the sort ever has happened to me, even though I may have, as you say, taken my eye off the road for a moment and had to correct the alignment of the car. I have never even in those circumstances swerved into a side road and I didn't on this occasion either.'

'Tell me, Mr Crane,' said counsel, 'have you ever met Mr Loudwater before?'

'Not so far as I know.'

'As far as you know, Mr Crane, has Mr Loudwater any reason in the world to have a grudge against you?'

'None at all.'

'There's no feud between your two families?'

'None whatever.'

'Then can you think why on earth Mr Loudwater should come into court and state on oath what he has stated?'

'I've no idea.'

'It can't be a mistake, can it?'

'I don't see how it can be.'

'So he must have invented or imagined it? Why should he do that?'

'You should ask him that.'

'Well, let me ask you this,' said counsel. 'Isn't it an inescapable conclusion from your evidence that, if nothing of the kind happened, Mr Loudwater is telling lies when he says he didn't know the plaintiff before or alternatively he has been offered some inducement to come to corroborate the plaintiff in court?'

'Surely that's a matter for argument, Mr Fergus,' said the judge. 'The witness' views on it don't help me in the least.'

'Do you suggest that Mr Loudwater has been bribed to give evidence?' asked counsel.

'I don't suggest anything,' said the defendant. 'I simply know that there was no accident of any kind on that occasion and that I did not swerve into any road off the London road on my way on that day.'

'Can you assist his Honour in any way,' asked counsel, 'to come to a decision as to whether you are speaking the truth on this matter rather than the plaintiff and Mr Loudwater?'

'Well, I was driving,' said the defendant, 'and I ought to know what happened.'

That concluded the defendant's evidence and counsel for the defendant then addressed the court.

'I respectfully submit,' he said, 'that the right way for your Honour to approach this case, which I agree is an unusual one, is to ask yourself whether you have confidence in the defendant's evidence. If you haven't, then I would respectfully agree that the plaintiff is entitled to judgment. But if you do have confidence in the defendant's evidence, you don't have to consider all the reasons why the plaintiff and his witness should have given the evidence that they have given. It is enough for your Honour to say, "I've heard this witness and he has in my view given evidence honestly and clearly and I believe him to be a man of complete integrity. He has never been in court before in his life, his attitude in cross-examination was that of an honest, careful man and I accept his word that he had no accident on this occasion." Your Honour is not deciding a criminal case and it is not for the defendant to establish his case either beyond all reasonable doubt or upon the probabilities. It is for the plaintiff to establish *his* case upon the probabilities, and if you find that the defendant is a witness of truth and that it is in the highest degree improbable that he could have made a mistake about such a matter then in my submission your Honour has to go no further. It is quite unnecessary to enquire how the action came to be brought. Accordingly, I respectfully submit that your Honour should find that the defendant was in fact an extremely reliable witness and, if your Honour does find that, I ask you to give judgment in his favour.'

Counsel sat down. Counsel for the plaintiff rose to reply.

'I submit, your Honour,' he said, 'that, although this case is a little unusual, it is not all that difficult. In your

Honour's experience at the Bar you must have heard many honest witnesses who felt quite certain that they were telling the truth in the witness box but who were in fact quite wrong. I suggest that this is the case here. My learned friend quite rightly says that you have to decide this case upon the probabilities and that it is for the plaintiff to show that the probabilities are on his side. I respectfully submit that only one question has to be asked by your Honour to satisfy yourself that the probabilities are very much on the side of the plaintiff. That question is this. Which is the more probable? That the defendant should have done something that everybody does, and made a mistake in his driving and in his recollection of what happened that day, or that two people who upon the evidence neither knew each other nor knew the defendant should put their heads together for no known reason to come and give false evidence before your Honour? I respectfully submit that there is only one possible answer to that question. Everyone in this case is of good character. Your Honour may decide that one witness gave a better account of himself in the witness box than another. I should be quite prepared to agree with my learned friend that the defendant *appeared* to be telling the truth and, indeed, I would be prepared to concede that he may well have believed that what he was saying was true. But what about the plaintiff and Mr Loudwater? Did they not also appear to be telling the truth? Your Honour cannot look into the hearts of these people. Your Honour can only judge them from your experience of human affairs and by the evidence which they actually gave in this court. If my client and Mr Loudwater were wrong in what they've said, they have been guilty of at least two criminal offences – conspiracy and perjury. On the other hand, if the defendant is wrong in what he says, I don't suggest that he's been guilty of any offence. The mistakes which honest people can make in everyday life are to your Honour's knowledge innumerable. I accept that it appears impossible to the defendant that he could have conducted such a manoeuvre while driving without remembering it, but can your Honour not remember cases where a witness has genuinely forgotten something far more striking than the defendant's manoeuvre?'

'If you ask me,' said Judge Rokeby, 'I can't at the moment. The accident only took place about six months ago and the claim was made on the defendant very shortly after the accident. It's a strange thing for the defendant to have forgotten.'

'I would accept that,' said counsel. '*Very* strange, if you like. But is it anything like as strange as that two respectable people would put their heads together to invent a story like this for the purpose of making a bit of money for one of them? After all, the damages at the most would run into a few hundred pounds. I ask the rhetorical question. Is it worthwhile to risk going to prison for perjury and conspiracy in order to make a few hundred pounds to be divided between two people? In my submission the question has only to be asked to provide its own answer. I venture to suggest to your Honour that, unless you can find some compelling reason for saying that you do not believe the plaintiff or Mr Loudwater, you are bound to come to a conclusion in the plaintiff's favour. I would respectfully ask your Honour, if you are minded to decide in favour of the defendant, to state in your judgment in detail the reasons why you do not accept the evidence of the plaintiff or Mr Loudwater. In my submission it is not enough for you to say, as my learned friend has submitted, that you accept the evidence of the defendant, and that you found him a truthful and trustworthy witness. In my submission, in this case that is not enough. In his case there is a possibility of a mistake. In the plaintiff's case there is no such possibility. Accordingly, before your Honour is entitled to find in favour of the defendant you have got to point to things in the plaintiff's or Mr Loudwater's evidence or the ways in which they respectively gave that evidence which make your Honour suspect – and I agree that would be enough – that they are not telling the truth. Unless your Honour can put your finger on a piece of evidence which they gave or on a particular way in which they gave certain parts of their evidence or – even though in my submission it would be very unreliable – a look on their faces as they gave their evidence – unless your Honour can point to some such reason for not accepting what they say, you are bound as a matter of law to come to a conclusion in favour of the plaintiff.'

Counsel sat down. The judge paused for a moment or two and then gave his judgment. Having stated the facts he went on, 'This is in my view a most unusual case. I must admit that I preferred the way in which the defendant gave his evidence to the way in which the plaintiff and Mr Loudwater gave their evidence. But counsel for the plaintiff is perfectly right in saying that in this case, before I come to a conclusion adverse to the plaintiff, I must be able to point to something in his evidence or Mr Loudwater's evidence which makes me suspect that they are not telling the truth and in my opinion it must be something concrete – not just a feeling or masculine intuition. The defendant is quite one of the best witnesses I've heard in an accident case. I could really find no fault with his evidence at all. His counsel suggests that that is enough to enable me to decide the case, but in my opinion it isn't. Were there no possibility that he could have been mistaken or were there some possibility that the plaintiff or Mr Loudwater could have been mistaken, the matter would have been different and I should have decided in the defendant's favour. Now there is no doubt that the plaintiff injured his toe and it is plain from the medical evidence that the injury to the toe was consistent with it having been run over by a car. It was also, I agree, consistent with his having been injured in some other way, even by his striking his foot against a wall or some other hard object. It is also a fact that the defendant was driving his car in the neighbourhood at the time of the alleged accident. Counsel for the plaintiff has rightly said that it is extremely improbable that two people of good character would put their heads together to make money out of an insurance company in this criminal way. It is, I agree, improbable that the defendant would have been involved in such an accident without his remembering it, but to decide this case it is sufficient to say that that is far less improbable than is the improbability that the plaintiff and Mr Loudwater should have been guilty of conspiracy and perjury. In my view that is enough to decide this case and there must be judgment for the plaintiff for damages which I understand have now been agreed at £400.'

After having given judgment, Judge Rokeby rose for the luncheon interval and he and his companion went into his private room.

'Well,' he said, 'what did you think of that? Did you agree with my decision?'

'I don't see how you could have decided otherwise, but personally I don't think the truth came out. I think the defendant was telling the truth and that this was a fraudulent claim, but nevertheless I should have decided in the same way as you, because there is wholly insufficient material on which to say that the claim is a fraudulent one. I wish I knew the truth because I don't believe that justice has been done.'

In the meantime the defendant was consulting with his counsel and Mr Philpot, his solicitor. 'Can I appeal?' he asked.

'You can appeal,' said counsel, 'but in my opinion you would have no earthly chance of succeeding on appeal. Indeed, if you had won, I think the plaintiff would have had more chance of upsetting that judgment than you would now have of upsetting this one.'

'How on earth can you say that?' asked Crane. 'You told me before we started that you believed what I said to be true.'

'I still do,' said counsel, 'but to find in your favour the judge had at least to suspect that this was a fraudulent conspiracy.'

'It must have been.'

'I daresay,' said counsel, 'but you didn't prove it.'

'I thought it was for the plaintiff to prove his case, not for me to disprove it.'

'I think he did prove it,' said counsel. 'It's a very odd case, but it was not enough for the judge to say he thought that you were a reliable witness. He had to give reasons for saying that he suspected the plaintiff and Mr Loudwater were real criminals. I cross-examined them as well as I could and, although I don't think either of them made a tremendously good impression on the judge, there was nothing on which I could put my finger which enabled me to submit that they were telling lies.'

'I must do something,' said the defendant.

'I'm afraid there's nothing you can do.'

'You don't seem to realise how frustrating it is,' said the defendant. 'It's not just my driving character that I'm worried about. It's the experience of having told the truth and not being believed.'

'If that's all that's worrying you,' said counsel, 'you can set your mind at rest. The judge certainly didn't disbelieve you. On the contrary, he said he accepted you as an honest witness. What he said was that it was more likely that you'd made a mistake than that the plaintiff and Loudwater were criminals. Can't you see for yourself that that's right?'

'It may be from the lawyer's point of view,' said the defendant, 'but from *my* point of view I have come to court and I have taken an oath and I have told the truth and I've nevertheless lost the case. The insurance company would have paid anyway. Why should I have gone to all this trouble unless I was in the right?'

'I think you were in the right,' said counsel, 'but it's simply one of those things. You must comfort yourself with the fact that the judge said you were a splendid witness.'

'Who's going to believe that,' said the defendant, 'when I have to add that I lost the case? It's like telling a man what a good chap he is and then sending him to prison for three years.'

'I'm very sorry,' said counsel. 'You can appeal if you wish, but you'll have to find the money for the costs yourself, as I'm quite sure that the insurance company won't do it. And I'm equally sure that you'll lose on appeal. In my view you haven't a hope of success.'

'Well, I don't care,' said the defendant, 'I can't live with this thing. I shall appeal.'

'You'll feel worse when you've lost it,' said counsel.

'At least,' said the defendant, 'I shall have done everything I can. If I don't appeal, I shall always wonder whether I would have won if I had.'

'My advice to you,' said counsel, 'is first of all not to appeal at all, but if you're determined to do something, then I suggest you conduct the appeal yourself. That will save you a certain amount of money, as you'll only have the other side's costs to pay when you've lost. In my opinion you would merely be throwing away money to employ your solicitors and me to argue the case for you.'

'Very well. I'll accept your advice on that, and I'm very grateful for it. No doubt the solicitors will tell me how I do appeal, because I don't know any of the technicalities of this sort of thing.'

'Of course they will,' said counsel. 'Mr Philpot will advise you as much as necessary and can even sit with you in court if you would like him to do so.'

'Assuredly,' said Mr Philpot.

Later on that day Julian telephoned the defendant's solicitors, said who he was and asked if he could speak to a partner. He was put through to Mr Philpot.

'I'm very sorry to trouble you, Mr Philpot,' he said, 'but I was present in court today when the case of the broken toe was heard. It looked to me as though the defendant was likely to appeal and I'd be most grateful if you could let me know when the appeal is likely to be heard, if there is one.'

'Assuredly, your Honour,' said Mr Philpot.

In consequence, six months later Julian was in court to hear Mr Crane open his appeal.

'My Lords,' he said after the case had been called on, 'I am appearing in this appeal myself and I ought to tell your Lordships that the reason that I have not got counsel appearing for me is because he has advised that the appeal has no chance of success.'

'That's a very frank way of opening the appeal,' said Lord Justice Broome, 'but it was quite unnecessary for you to tell us that and I can assure you that it won't prejudice our approach to the case. You tell us in your own words why the learned judge was wrong to give the plaintiff damages.'

'Because the accident never happened,' said Crane. 'I have always been told that the law was expensive but that it was fair and I say that it can't be fair if a man takes an oath to tell the truth, tells the truth and nevertheless loses his case.'

'It depends what the truth is,' said Lord Justice Stoop. 'A man may think he is legally in the right and tell the truth from beginning to end but the court may rightly decide that, although he has told the truth, the truth shows that the other side is entitled to win the case.'

'I don't know about that,' said Crane, 'but, if the truth is that the plaintiff's toe was never injured by my car, it would be a very odd kind of law which said he was entitled to get damages out of me.'

'You say that there never was an accident,' said Lord Justice Broome.

'There wasn't an accident in which I was concerned,' said Crane. 'Another car may have run over the plaintiff's toe or he may have injured it in some other way, but I was not concerned with it.'

'Surely it can't have been another car,' said Lord Justice Stoop. 'The plaintiff took the number of your car. You were in fact in the neighbourhood at the time the plaintiff says you ran over his toe. It really would be an impossible coincidence for another car with a different number to have gone through the same manoeuvre as the plaintiff says you did and for the plaintiff to have taken down the number of the wrong car. You aren't suggesting that's a real possibility, are you?'

'All I can say,' said Crane, 'is that I was never concerned in such an accident. I agree that the plaintiff injured his toe but that was nothing to do with me. I don't know if all your Lordships drive cars but, if you do, I am sure you will agree that it is impossible for a motorist to forget that he has swerved into a side turning and swerved out of it again.'

'I think I've forgotten more things than I remember,' said Lord Justice Anstey.

'But not within a day or two,' put in Lord Justice Broome. 'The claim was made within a day or two of the date of the accident and Mr Crane says that he couldn't have forgotten conducting such an unusual manoeuvre within a few days of having conducted it. I think there's a lot to be said for that.'

'I agree there's a lot to be said for it,' said Lord Justice Stoop, 'but this is only the one side of the case. Let us say that it is not at all likely that the appellant could have forgotten such a manoeuvre in such a short time. But is it impossible? No one who is aware of what tricks memory plays could say that it was impossible. But now look on the other side of the case. It is impossible that the plaintiff and his witness could have made a mistake. They were either substantially telling the truth or they concocted the story. I agree it is not impossible that they concocted the story. There are wicked people about and it is conceivable that the plaintiff and Mr Loudwater are two of them, but they are people of good character and all the learned judge said in effect was that it was less likely that people of good character would make up such a story and, fearing neither God nor regarding man, bring a fraudulent claim against the appellant than that the appellant by some trick of the memory should either have forgotten or not noticed that he had driven slightly into a side road and out again.'

'It was the unjust judge, wasn't it,' put in Lord Justice Anstey, 'who feared not God neither regarded man?'

'Well,' said Lord Justice Stoop, 'I certainly don't regard the appellant as the equivalent of the importunate widow. He made a very good impression indeed upon the learned judge in the court below and I'm not surprised, because he certainly makes a very good impression on me.'

'Thank you,' said Crane, 'but all the compliments in the world are not of much use to me if I'm still not believed when I tell the truth. Surely, if all your Lordships and Judge Rokeby find an honest man telling the truth, surely the law is not so stupid that it can't decide in my favour?'

'The law is not perfect,' said Lord Justice Broome. 'A man may in fact be in the right and yet lose his case for lack of evidence or by reason of some mistake made by his legal advisers or by reason of some mistake made by the judge. None of us is perfect or anything like it and some of us are very far from perfect. We do the best we can, but we are only human and we all make mistakes. No judge who has sat on the Bench for any time could put his hand on his heart and say that he felt sure that he'd never perpetrated any injustice. I am quite sure that I must have.'

'Why are they called Courts of Justice then?'

'I am sure that Judge Rokeby does justice in most of his cases,' said Lord Justice Anstey. 'We certainly try to do justice in all of ours, but human beings are fallible and all of them make mistakes from time to time.'

'But there is no need to make a mistake in *this* case,' said Crane. 'I've put my case fairly to you and I told Judge Rokeby the same.'

'Apart from judicial mistakes,' said Lord Justice Anstey, 'there may be cases where injustice is done because the law itself is not perfect. There is no means at the disposal of human courts by which the truth can be ascertained for certain and accordingly we have to have rules, which on the whole work fairly. One of those rules in civil cases is that in the normal way a case must be decided upon the probabilities. Although it is probable that somebody did something, it is not certain that he did. And in some cases he didn't do it. I will assume that your case is one of them. And if you didn't do it, you would certainly suffer an injustice if the judgment of the court below is upheld by us. But what else are we to do? Every legal machine has to have a set of rules by which the wheels go round and the relevant rule in your case is what may be called the probability rule. Don't you agree yourself that it is in the highest degree improbable that for the sake of £200 apiece two respectable men would conspire to cheat your insurance company?'

'It was unlikely that Jack the Ripper would kill all those people,' said Crane, 'but he did.'

'That was quite different,' said Lord Justice Anstey. 'In those cases women were actually murdered. The only question was who had murdered them. The question in your case is whether a crime was committed at all. Do you dispute that it is highly unlikely that reputable people would commit such a crime?'

'Isn't it just as unlikely,' said Crane, 'that I should run over a man's toe and then lie about it? I'm a reputable person too, I hope.'

'Certainly,' said Lord Justice Broome. 'It is just as unlikely. Possibly even more unlikely in your case and nobody suggests that you have lied about it. The whole point of the case is that, however unlikely it may be, it is possible that you are mistaken.'

'I am not mistaken, my Lord.'

'I certainly believe that you don't think you are,' said Lord Justice Broome, 'but that isn't enough for you to win this appeal. You must satisfy us that you can't be mistaken.'

'Well,' said Lord Justice Anstey; 'it is, as the learned judge said, a very odd case but, as far as I am concerned, I am afraid there is nothing more that this court can do about it. You're a sensible man and you must try to put it out of your mind.'

'How on earth can I do that? I can't live with it.'

'Now, Mr Crane,' said Lord Justice Broome, 'that's foolish talk. People have had to live with far worse injustices than you'll have to live with. Why, some people have even been wrongly convicted of crime and actually served sentences of imprisonment. That was far worse for them than this is for you. You must comfort yourself with the fact that this is an imperfect world and that even courts of justice are not perfect. We all strive to attain absolute justice but we know that it is not attainable. Is there anything else that you wish to say?'

'It doesn't seem any use,' said Crane.

'I'm afraid it isn't,' said Lord Justice Stoop. 'You told us in the beginning that your learned counsel had advised you that this appeal had no hope of success.'

'I thought you weren't going to take any notice of that,' said Crane.

'We didn't,' said Lord Justice Stoop, 'while we were considering the appeal, but now that all of us have come to exactly the same conclusion and for the same reasons, although we put it out of our minds during the appeal, we can't have forgotten it.'

'Any more than I could have forgotten swerving into the side of the road,' said Crane.

A few minutes later the appeal was dismissed with costs and the disconsolate Crane walked out of court. As he was walking along the corridor Julian came up to him.

'My name is Julian Whitehill,' he said. 'I used to be a circuit judge. I heard your case in the County Court and

I've just listened to it in the Court of Appeal. I wonder if I
might have a word with you?'

'Certainly. It's very good of you to take an interest.'

'Let's sit down here,' said Julian, 'and have a chat about
it.'

They sat on one of the benches. 'First of all I want to
offer you my sympathy. But I know that isn't any use to
you. I firmly believe that you've suffered an injustice
today.'

'Then why didn't I win my appeal?'

'You couldn't, for reasons which the judges explained.
There wasn't enough evidence. On the facts before the
judge and the Court of Appeal you were bound to lose.
But I don't believe you ever had that accident and, if you
are agreeable, I'm going to try to investigate the matter. I'd
like to have a chat with you first.'   .

'*You* are going to investigate the matter?'

'Only if you'd like me to.'

'But how can you do it?'

'We'll come to that a little later on. First of all I want to
have a chat with you to clear my own mind about it. I
believe that there was a conspiracy by these two
scallywags, but what I still don't understand and what
we've got to investigate is why they did it.'

'To make a bit of money, surely?'

'Four hundred pounds!' said the judge. 'That's not
enough. Counsel was perfectly right in submitting that it
is most unlikely that people without previous convictions
would risk doing a thing like that for such a small sum of
money. So what conclusion does that lead us to?'

'You tell me.'

'If you're in the right,' said Julian, 'and I believe you are,
this case must be only one of a number. That would make
sense. There must be a conspiracy by some people to find

men and women who've recently injured themselves, to take the numbers of cars and then to invent a story about an accident. There must be somebody who knows about the law involved. All they have to do is to find an injured person who is prepared to take part in it and then to find a potential criminal who has never been caught to corroborate the circumstances of the alleged accident. This will require a good bit of organisation.'

'Are you proposing to go to the police?'

'Not at the moment. They're extremely busy and, unless one can give them some material to work upon, there is really nothing they can do.'

'Well, what is your suggestion?'

'I'm going to employ someone to investigate the matter.'

'May I know who?'

'You wouldn't know him. He's a man called Mountjoy. He's the only completely reliable enquiry agent I've ever come across. He's highly intelligent, absolutely trustworthy and enjoys making bricks with the minimum of straw.'

Julian had first met Mountjoy when he was at the Bar. Although counsel does not usually see witnesses, in one case with which Julian was concerned there were special circumstances which made it desirable that Mountjoy should come to his chambers. The first impression he made on Julian was not a good one. Mountjoy was then a youngish man, full of bounce and confidence and with the patter of a fast-moving salesman. He spoke at length and quickly and liberally peppered most of his statements with such phrases as 'I'll tell you the truth' and 'to be perfectly honest' and 'I won't tell you a lie', which are often the signs that a person is not telling the truth, is not perfectly honest and *is* telling a lie. Strangely enough, as the judge eventually discovered, this was not so in the case of Mountjoy. He was absolutely reliable and, if he said that he personally saw a husband in a divorce case clamber out of a window on the third floor of a house and let himself down to the ground by a drainpipe, that is what in fact happened, although the husband was not a burglar by trade and did not enjoy climbing down drainpipes. As it turned out, he enjoyed even less the prospect of being beaten up by another husband whose wife he had been visiting. Mountjoy was also extremely good at getting into touch with the people whom he was shadowing, and even gaining their confidence. In one industrial fraud case, where the people whom he was employed to watch were passing off scented water as a very expensive drug, he actually supplied the criminals with marked cartons, so that eventually, when the police were informed and the chief suspect's house searched, they were found on the premises. Julian felt reasonably certain that, if any man could discover the truth of the matter, Mountjoy could.

CHAPTER FOUR

Successful Search

Peter Mountjoy was a somewhat unusual person. He was born of a poor and anything but humble father, who had been a highly militant shop steward. However, in spite of his revolutionary sentiments, which he expressed freely and colourfully, he was liked by his employers almost as much as by those whom he represented. This was chiefly because he was a man of his word. They knew that he never bluffed and that, if he said that his men were going to strike, they were going to do so. Equally, if he said that he hoped that he would be able to arrange a compromise, they knew that he would do his best to achieve one. It is a great advantage to an employer to know almost for certain what his men are going to do. It enables him to plan accordingly. Mountjoy's father was what might be termed a moderate revolutionary. He never suggested that his employers should be put against a wall and shot; only that their incomes should be reduced by nine-tenths and that they should be made to work hard for them.

Peter (known to most of his friends as PM) had inherited his father's honesty and sense of humour. Before the 1939-45 war he had been a bus conductor, where his qualities made him the equal of the really well-mannered conductors, who never abuse their power. It is a great pity that there are some who do. In the 1939-45 war PM had been in the infantry. During active operations it was his regular jest when a shell was heard·to be coming in his direction to ring an imaginary bell three times and say, 'No room here; full up.' During a particularly heavy bombardment he was eventually picked up, still just conscious, with only one leg. As he was taken away by the stretcher-bearers, he was heard to remark faintly, 'Another one behind.'

The absence of a leg made it impossible for him to continue on the buses after the war. Before becoming a bus conductor he had tried his hand at being a professional conjuror, but, although his patter was excellent, his performance was not. Like many people with agile brains he had hands which were far from agile. On the last occasion when he acted as a conjuror he invited some members of the audience to step up to assist him with one of his tricks. He wanted one member as a guinea-pig and two to see fair play.

'I'll tell you the truth,' he said to the audience. 'I'm not relying for this trick upon any confederate. I admit, to be perfectly honest, that sometimes I do. I plant a friend among the audience and sometimes I even rely upon the good nature of a complete stranger. For example, I spread out a number of cards on the table, get half a dozen complete strangers up from the audience, and say that I will go off the stage and that during my absence the members of the audience on the stage are to look at one or more cards or none and that when I come back I will tell them accurately what's happened. I show that there are no mirrors anywhere and that I cannot possibly see what card, if any, is turned up. As I go out I whisper to the last man, "When I come to a card which has been touched, cough", and then I go straight out. I have never yet met a stranger who let me down over that. But this time I'm not using any confederate and, so that you can be quite satisfied about that, I'm going to send these gentlemen back to their seats and ask you to elect your own representatives.' Eventually three other people came on to the stage. 'Now, this is a very simple little trick,' he said, 'but it looks impossible. I have here some iced water and I'm going to take a dessert spoonful of it and pour it down the neck of the gentleman who's kindly volunteered to be a victim. He will be neither cold nor wet as a result. Now I do hope that you are all satisfied that none of these gentlemen is a confederate, particularly the gentleman who has so kindly sacrificed his back in aid of my performance.'

He then picked up a spoon, filled it with iced water and invited the two umpires to feel it with their fingers. 'Would you kindly assure the audience, gentlemen, that this is both liquid and cold.' The assurance was duly given. Then he approached the victim.

'Have you ever seen me before in your life?' he asked.

'Never.'

'Right,' said PM. 'Feeling nervous?' he asked the victim.

'Not in the least.'

'That's because you trust me.'

'Absolutely.'

'My wife does too,' said PM, 'and she's never had cause to regret it. I hope you won't.'

'I'm sure I won't,' said the victim.

'All right,' said PM. 'That's enough of the chat. Let's get down to business. Come with me, gentlemen, please,' and the three of them walked towards the centre of the platform.

The trick was indeed a simple one. The spoon was not in fact a genuine ordinary spoon at all, although at a casual glance it looked like one. Just as he was about to pour its contents down the back of the volunteer, PM would press a hidden spring at the back of the spoon and the water would be sucked into the stem. So that the members of the audience on the stage would not notice this, he would divert their attention at the critical moment either to something else on the stage or to the audience. Unfortunately, however, on the last occasion when he had performed the trick he had by accident picked up an ordinary spoon, with the result that a spoonful of ice-cold water went down the back of the victim. He leapt up angry and wet, but PM, entirely ignoring his behaviour, turned calmly to the audience and said: 'Now, sir, will you please assure the audience that the water really did go down. D'you remember what I said at the beginning? He won't complain, I said. He won't feel a thing. He won't mind at all. He won't even feel wet.' The audience, observing the obvious discomfort and extreme anger of the victim, was convulsed with laughter. PM bowed to them and then, after the manner of a conductor, motioned to the angry man to take his bow. He had seen no alternative but to rely upon his good nature. But this was more than good nature could stand. When asked to take his bow, the victim rushed at PM and struck him to the ground. As he was lying there, he was heard by the first few rows of the audience to say somewhat faintly: 'You see, ladies and gentlemen, I assured you that he was not a confederate.'

So he gave up conjuring and became a bus conductor.

For the purpose of his job as a conjuror he had taken pains to cure his cockney accent, with the result that in the end he was like an educated Scotsman, that is to say, he could speak with an Oxford or cockney accent at will, just as the educated Scot can speak pure English or broad Scots.

After the war he married a nice girl called Beatrice. His father and mother called her 'Beetrice', as he did when he was with them. Otherwise he called her 'Beertrice', until he suddenly hit on the idea of calling her 'Annie'.

'It's too good to miss,' he said. 'Then we shall be PM and AM. Twenty-four hours between us.'

In spite of the loss of his leg, PM was as cheerful as he was before the war. It may be that one day medical science will progress so far that doctors will fully understand the exact function of each minute brain cell. Had they been able to do that in PM's day and had he left his body to the nation, they would have been able to show his pickled brain as a fine example of *homo felix*.

For some time after the war he was a salesman. Although his artificial leg very slightly impeded his activities, the advantage he got from the natural sympathy which people showed to a man who had lost a leg in the war easily outweighed that disadvantage. And his excellent patter stood him in good stead. He would have remained a salesman, if he had not by pure chance gone to a house where, unknown to the police, an escaped bank-robber was living. Going in the middle of the day, he expected to find only the wife at home, but the fact that the husband was there also did not at first raise any suspicions in his mind. The mere fact that a man remains at home during the normal hours of work and does not appear to be ill is not sufficient by itself, even in these days of lawlessness, to make the ordinary person suspect that he's up to no good. However, PM was a little surprised at the ease with which he sold quite an expensive electric product and at the fact that he was immediately paid in full in cash. He also noticed that the husband did not remain in the room for more than about half a minute and that the wife appeared anxious to get rid of their visitor as soon as possible. The simplest way of doing this was to buy the article and pay for it, and this she did. PM had never achieved such a quick sale and on reflection he thought it advisable to report the matter to the police. In consequence, the man was arrested and PM had to give evidence against him. He was congratulated by the judge both on the way in which he gave his evidence and upon his extreme good sense in reporting the matter to the police. The Commissioner of Police also sent him a special letter thanking him for what he had done. The letter said that but for his disability and his age the Commissioner would have been delighted for him to come into the Police Force and added that, if he had done so, he thought he would have risen to a very high rank indeed.

As PM did not think that he had really done very much at all, he wondered if he could lead a more interesting life and a more remunerative one if he became a private investigator. He was independent as a salesman and could carry out his duties in his own time. So, while continuing to act as a salesman for most of his time, he spent a little money on advertising his services as a private investigator, with the determination that, if he succeeded, he would give up selling goods altogether and that, if he failed, he would return to that occupation full time.

His first jobs as a detective were the pedestrian ones of watching erring husbands. It was during a case resulting from his enquiries and observations that Julian as a judge came across him. His catchphrases again at first made a bad impression on the judge, and when during his evidence in answer to a question he said, 'I'll tell you the truth,' the judge interrupted with, 'You've already sworn to do that.'

'I know, my Lord,' said PM, 'that's one of the reasons why I'm going to tell it. If I didn't tell the truth, I shouldn't be any good at this job. If your butcher's meat is tender, you go back to him for more. If it isn't, you go somewhere else. There's only one way, my Lord, of always being believed and that is always telling the truth.'

'I wish everyone who gave evidence in front of me thought the same.'

'Quite frankly, my Lord, I'm glad a lot of my colleagues don't. Otherwise the competition would be too great. A little inconclusive true evidence is far more effective in my experience, my Lord, than a lot of false conclusive evidence.'

'Thank you, Mr Mountjoy,' said Julian. 'I'd be glad if you'd confine your further remarks to the facts of the case.'

'Point taken, my Lord,' said PM.

When PM received a letter from Julian saying that he would like to employ him professionally he was delighted. 'Hope it isn't about his own affairs though,' he said. 'He seemed a decent sort of a chap.'

'Is he coming to see you?' said AM.

'One day, I hope, but not the first time. I must wait on his Honour. Funny, when I first appeared in front of him he was his Lordship. Now he's only his Honour. It must be rather nice to be called my Lord.'

'Pity you didn't go in for it,' said AM, 'or you would have been.'

'I might,' said PM. 'To judge from some of the counsel I come across the competition isn't all that great.'

'You do think a lot of yourself, don't you.'

'If I don't, who's going to? And I think a lot more of you.'

'You can't. I'm so stupid.'

'Some of the stupidest people are the nicest,' said PM, 'and you're one of them.'

'D'you really think I'm stupid?' said AM.

'That's what I liked about you from the start. D'you know what I thought when I first saw you? I thought you were the prettiest, stupidest girl I'd ever seen.'

'D'you like me being stupid then?'

'Of course I do. You can't have brains on both sides of the family. We'd be quarrelling all the time. Brains aren't the important thing in a marriage. It's the nature of the beast.'

'Now you're calling me a beast.'

'I'm calling us both beasts. Beasts or animals. No, it's the nature that matters, not brains. You've got a sweet face and a sweet nature and I don't think I could love anybody as much as I love you. Would you like it in writing?'

'I've got it,' said AM. 'I've kept all your letters.'

Punctually at the agreed time PM arrived at Julian's house and was soon sitting with him in his study. Julian told him what the problem was and then went on, 'There seem to me one or two possibilities which we've got to eliminate. We must first make sure that the solicitors employed by the plaintiff were not themselves involved. It's improbable that they were, but we must eliminate the possibility. If, as I strongly suspect, they are not involved, then you'll have to find out who is the person or who are the persons who are running this fraud. That will be much more difficult to ascertain. Of course, conversely, if as a result of your enquiries it appears that the broken toe case was the only one, then my suspicions would be unfounded. But I do not believe that, if the claim is a dishonest one, it can have been the only example. It simply wouldn't be worth it. Well, how are you going to set about it?'

'Wouldn't it be better if you left that to me, your Honour? I can't break the law but enquiry agents sometimes have to do things judges wouldn't do or mightn't approve of and it might be better for them not to know in advance.'

'I must take full responsibility for whatever you do,' said Julian, 'so I might as well know what I'm letting myself in for. And you must promise not to do anything of which I might disapprove.'

'I'd hate to do that. It might limit my activities.'

'I'll be as broadminded as I can, but you must tell me what you propose to do. If you want to take a step which you think is questionable you must get my authority to take it first. Now, how do you propose to tackle the solicitors or do you want to think it over first?'

'Well, I suppose the simplest way would be to go to them and say that I've got a wife or a relative who's got an injury claim in respect of an accident but that unfortunately we haven't any witnesses. First of all, I shall see what the reaction is and eventually I shall ask whether they can provide a witness. But I'll have to lead up to that very carefully.'

'You will also have to go to the police first,' said Julian, 'and say what you're going to do or you may be charged with attempting to pervert the course of justice.'

'This is exactly what I had in mind,' said PM. 'I don't for a moment expect them to agree to my suggestions in the first instance, but, if they don't communicate with the police about them, it will be strong evidence to show that at least it's a pretty questionable firm. Any respectable solicitor who's asked if he could find a witness by bribery would surely be bound to report the matter to the police.'

'Certainly, but if the man you interview is intelligent, he will pretend to fall in with your suggestion and arrange another interview which can be heard by the police. If he's not so intelligent, he will refuse indignantly to do anything of the kind that you've suggested and ring the police in your presence.'

'But if he's crooked, he won't want to have anything to do with the police. It will be a little too near home and he will simply send me packing. I can't believe that he'd be so stupid to agree to the suggestion when it's made by a person about whom he knows nothing whatever.'

'I think you're probably right. Suppose as a result of your interview they're eliminated, what will you do next?'

'The only other two people I can start off with are the plaintiff and Loudwater. I'll start with one of them. If I can satisfy myself either that it was a genuine case or that it definitely wasn't, I'll come back to you, your Honour. If it was a genuine case, I'll simply ask for my fee and that will be that. If it was not genuine, then I'll tell you what I suggest and ask for your approval.' .

'That reminds me,' said Julian. 'What about the fee?'

'It all depends how long it takes. As I expect your Honour knows, we charge mainly by time plus expenses. I have no idea how long this case will take.'

'I follow that, but I can't just give you a blank cheque. Don't go above a hundred pounds, please, without coming to me for fresh instructions.'

'Very good, your Honour. Of course I'd do it for nothing if your Honour would let me have your name on my prospectus as one of my clients. I don't imagine you'd agree to that?'

'I'm afraid not,' said Julian.

'Very well then, I'll be as economical as I can, your Honour. I'm very flattered that your Honour should want to employ me at all. I'll get on with it at once.'

Soon afterwards PM left the judge and went to a telephone-box. He telephoned the solicitors – Torrid Harting – and made an appointment for two days later.

Then he went to Scotland Yard and asked for an interview with an inspector in the Fraud Squad.

After PM had explained what he intended to do, the inspector was silent for about half a minute and then said, 'How am I to know that you're genuine?'

'What d'you mean? Of course I'm genuine.'

'So you say, but how am I to know it?'

'I wouldn't have come to you if I weren't, would I?'

'Yes, you might have. Suppose you in fact wanted to bring a bogus action but want to protect yourself in case it doesn't come off? Wouldn't it be a simple thing to do to go to the police first, say what you're proposing to do, then if it comes off and the solicitors do as you ask, we shall never hear anything more about it but, on the other hand, if they are not prepared to do as you ask, you won't get into any sort of trouble. Then you can keep on doing the same thing until eventually some solicitor complies with your wishes and we hear nothing about it.'

'To tell you the truth,' said PM, 'that hadn't occurred to me. It's not half a bad idea, but I can assure you that isn't happening in my case.'

'How am I to know?'

'I suppose you can't for sure,' said PM. 'But what I am about to do is perfectly legal, so you can't prevent my doing it.'

'Oh, can't I?' said the inspector. 'Suppose I ring up Messrs. Torrid & Harting and tell them all about it now?'

'As a police officer, you shouldn't,' said PM. 'I don't expect they're crooks, but, if by chance they were, you would be preventing them from being caught and that isn't the job of the police.'

'But supposing *you* are a crook?' said the inspector. 'How am I to find out about you? I can't tell what other solicitors you may go to after you've been to these. You could go to hundreds and, if a hundred and ninety-nine out of two hundred won't help you, the two hundredth may.'

'Well, if I tell you that I'm prepared to put into writing that neither I nor any relative or friend of mine has had any accident in respect of which compensation is going to be sought, you can use that against me if you find that I or someone I'm acting for is claiming compensation.'

'We can't enquire from every court in the country,' said the inspector, 'as to whether you're involved in any proceedings there, and it might not come to proceedings. The insurance company might pay without the issue of a summons or the issue of a writ. Meantime, you're covered for every case where you're reported.'

'I think we can get over that. I tell you that I'm not going to any solicitors except Messrs Torrid & Harting, certainly not at the moment. If I do propose to go to any others, that will be because I will have got some further information which justifies it and, before going to them, I'll come back to you. In consequence, if any solicitor makes a complaint about me other than Torrid & Harting or any other person I've mentioned to you, you can take it that I'm not genuine. Now how can I get out of that?'

'Suppose Torrid & Harting don't report the matter?'

'Ah,' said PM, 'that's the whole point. I cannot conceive that an honest solicitor would not report it and in consequence, if they don't report it, I shall know pretty well that they were parties to the fraud which I believe to have taken place. If they do report it, I shan't have been to any other solicitors unless I tell you and I don't suppose that will arise. If it does, however, you will know all about it.'

'How will I know all about it?'

'Because I shall tell you.'

'Very well,' said the inspector, 'I think that's reasonably satisfactory. I'll notify them here that, if Torrid & Harting get on to us, the call should be put through to me and I will also notify the local police station.'

Two days later PM attended an interview with Mr Groaner, who was practising as Torrid & Harting.

'Do you do accident cases?' was his first question.

'Certainly,' said Mr Groaner. 'Is it a street or an industrial accident?'

'Street.'

'May I ask how you came to consult us?'

'I saw your name on the door, as a matter of fact.'

'Did you have the accident yourself?'

'Oh no, it was a friend of my wife's.'

'Was she driving or a pedestrian?'

'A pedestrian.'

'Was she hurt?'

'Some nasty bruising but no bones broken. But the trouble is that she's not young.'

'How old?'

'About seventy. Badly shocked.'

'How did it happen?'

'She was walking across a pedestrian crossing – she's very careful and always uses them – when, as she almost reached the end, a car came past and the wing caught her and sent her flying.'

'Were the police called?'

'No.'

'Why not? It was a pedestrian crossing.'

'That's why I've come to consult you in advance, because the trouble is that there were no witnesses.'

'Did the car stop?'

'No. Fortunately it wasn't going very fast and she was able to take his number.'

'Who picked her up?'

'She had to get up herself because there was no one there.'

'Was she definitely on the pedestrian crossing when she was knocked down?'

'Oh yes, but the driver might not have noticed it. It was at night and a wing just caught her. Or it might have been the bumper, I suppose. At any rate some part of the car caught her and sent her flying on to the pavement.'

'Has she made a claim yet?'

'No. We wanted to consult someone first.'

'Did you report the matter to the police?'

'No. We thought we'd better wait about that until we'd consulted someone. Because you see the driver mightn't have noticed.'

'The first thing to do,' said Mr Groaner, 'is to find out who was the owner of the car. If you'll give me the number, I'll make enquiries.'

PM started to feel in all his pockets. 'Here it is,' he said. 'Oh dear, I'm so sorry. That's a bus ticket. Just a moment. I know I've got it with me.' He felt in all his pockets one after the other. 'Ah, here we are – oh no, it isn't,' he said. 'I'm terribly sorry, to be perfectly honest, I must have left it behind. What I wanted to know in the first place before we started proceedings is what chance of success she has – without any witnesses.'

'She's sure the car knocked her down, is she, and she couldn't possibly have slipped?'

'She says so,' said PM. 'But it would have been nice if we could have had a witness to corroborate it.'

'It certainly would,' said Mr Groaner.

'You couldn't find one, I suppose?' said PM.

'Advertise, d'you mean?'

'Are there any other ways?'

'Well,' said Mr Groaner, 'we could send somebody to make enquiries at the neighbouring houses to see if anybody happened to see the accident. It's unlikely, though, because, if they did, they would have come to help, wouldn't they?'

'She wouldn't want to take proceedings unless she was almost certain of success. If only there'd been a witness I suppose she would be.'

'Would be what?'

'Certain of success.'

'It depends on the witness,' said Mr Groaner, 'but I expect so. The judge would ask himself which is the more likely. That a driver didn't notice just catching an old lady in the dark or that an independent witness should say something that he knew to be untrue. No, if there were a witness who definitely saw it, you'd be pretty well bound to win. But I don't see how there can have been one.'

'Not if you can't find one,' said PM.

'D'you want us to advertise?' said Mr Groaner. 'I can't pretend I've got much hope that it'll produce anything. As I said, it doesn't look as though there was a witness.'

'I did read somewhere, Mr Groaner, about something called a professional witness. Could you tell me what that is?'

'A professional witness? A doctor or an engineer or something of that sort?'

'No, I mean a professional witness of accidents. You couldn't find one of those, I suppose?'

Mr Groaner laughed. 'I have known of such cases,' he said. 'People who've heard a bang and looked up and like the idea of going into court and telling their story in the witness box and with luck making a joke which the Press will report. But judges are pretty scared of them on the whole. I do remember one case, though, where a chap volunteered to give evidence for one side or the other. I forget which but that doesn't matter. He turned out to have eight previous convictions for burglary and housebreaking. After the result in that case my advice to my clients,' said Mr Groaner with a laugh, 'is that, if they want an independent witness, they should choose somebody without any previous convictions for burglary and housebreaking.'

'You mean,' said PM, 'that the side that called that man lost the case?'

'I do indeed,' said Mr Groaner.

'Well, what would you advise in this case?' asked PM.

'I should have to see the client first, then I could make some judgment as to whether she's likely to win the case on her own evidence. If she's quite definite and if she's a good witness, she very well might.'

'I'm afraid she won't be a very good witness,' said PM. 'She stammers.'

'That wouldn't matter,' said Mr Groaner.

'And she's got a very bad memory. How soon would the case come on?'

'Let me see. We could bring it in the County Court and, if the defendant doesn't pay after the claim has been made, I think we could get it on in about two months.'

'Two months?' said PM, in a somewhat horrified tone. 'I'm afraid she'll have forgotten everything by then.'

'Well, we might get it on in six weeks,' said Mr Groaner.

'A lot of the trouble with her is that she's very nervous and would be liable to agree with everything she's asked in cross-examination. She's never been in court before and hates the idea of it.'

'It looks to me,' said Mr Groaner, 'that, if your client has only been bruised, she'd better forget the whole thing.'

'Widespread bruising,' said PM. 'But supposing she'd been really badly injured, I mean broken bones, ruptured spleen and all that sort of thing, shortening of life, what could we have done then?'

'Well, in those cases,' said Mr Groaner, 'where the damages could be very heavy, you may get a reasonable settlement out of an insurance company. But there's not much point in discussing that sort of case. Your friend was only bruised.'

'Could she get legal aid, do you think?' asked PM.

'It depends how much money she's got. Does she own the house she lives in?'

'Yes.'

'Is there any mortgage on it?'

'No, I don't think so.'

'Then I doubt if she could. Legal aid is very useful and it's enabled a lot of people to be properly represented when otherwise they couldn't have been. But they are all people with low incomes and practically no capital. The rich and the poor are all right. It's the wretched man in the middle who gets into difficulties and the costs of litigation are no joke, I assure you. Even though they haven't gone up as other things have.'

'What does a witness get paid?'

'It depends on what he is,' said Mr Groaner. 'I take it you're not talking about expert witnesses? They're in a different category.'

'Oh no. Just an ordinary witness.'

'He gets his expenses on a reasonable scale and a reasonable amount for loss of time.'

'Does he ever get a bonus when the case is done?'

'Not from me,' said Mr Groaner, 'but I shouldn't be surprised if a satisfied plaintiff or defendant doesn't show his appreciation in the usual way.'

'Is there anything wrong in it?'

'No,' said Mr Groaner, 'provided you're not asking a man to commit perjury, there's nothing legally wrong in promising to give a man money to give evidence but, if the fact were known, it wouldn't do the side who promised the money very much good.'

'Have you ever known a case where a man who wasn't really a witness was bribed to say that he was?'

'I've suspected it sometimes,' said Mr Groaner, 'but I've never known for certain.'

'How interesting,' said PM. 'Not recently, by any chance?'

'I'm afraid,' said Mr Groaner, 'that I don't talk about one client's case to another client.'

'I'm sorry,' said PM. 'I do apologise. I'm afraid I couldn't resist the temptation to ask questions on the subject. I'm very interested in it. How much do I owe you?'

'If you go to the outer office,' said Mr Groaner, 'you can pay them there. They'll know how much.'

In PM's attaché case which he took with him to the interview with the solicitor was a tape-recorder. So he was able to give Julian a full account of what had happened. Julian listened to the recording three times.

'I think you did very well,' he said, 'and that we can be reasonably certain that the solicitors were not in the fraud. Truth has a nasty habit of coming out. In my view, truth nearly always makes sense. When a man is lying, usually if he's questioned enough on the subject he will say something, even something quite small, which doesn't fit in. Truth is a jigsaw puzzle and all the pieces are there if you can find them. It's when you find the odd piece that doesn't fit in anywhere that you can be pretty certain that you are not dealing with the truth. Both at the Bar and on the Bench I nearly always found that, when my client or a witness said something unintelligible or something which did not make sense, the reason was because he had lied about the matter. There is nothing in your interview with Mr Groaner which doesn't make sense. So I think we've got to move on.'

'Who shall I try next?' asked PM. 'Broad or Loudwater?'

'On the whole I should say Loudwater,' said Julian. 'Now, if I'm not wrong in my belief, he must be in the swindle. If with your interviews with him you don't bring out something which doesn't make sense, then the probability is that my very strong belief in his guilt is wrong. But I think you will find something, although it will probably take a little time.'

'Very well, your Honour,' said PM. 'I'll start today. But I must tell the police that Groaner is in the clear.'

Julian was well aware that in many aspects of human life there is no such thing as absolute truth. In many cases what appears to be true to one person genuinely appears to be false to another. But although some philosophers would say that this applied to everything, for practical purposes there are many cases where a man can safely act upon the assumption that this is true and that is false. If that were not so, courts of justice could hardly carry on their business at all. The truth about the cause of an accident very often never comes to light and Julian believed that as soon as the courts ceased to pursue the slippery eel of truth in that sphere the better. He had once had a case where he simply could not make up his mind whether the plaintiff or the defendant was at fault. The witnesses on both sides appeared to be trustworthy. They gave their evidence clearly and well. The plaintiff and his witnesses said that *he* was on the proper side of the white line and the defendant and his witnesses said that he was on the proper side of the white line. Julian in his judgment said that he didn't know who was on the proper side of the white line and, accordingly, as the plaintiff had not proved that the defendant was on the wrong side of the line and the defendant had not proved that the plaintiff was on the wrong side of the line, the claim and counterclaim both failed. Both sides appealed from this judgment and the Court of Appeal in its wisdom said in effect that the judge was paid to make up his mind and that, if he didn't, he wasn't earning his keep. It sent the case back to be retried by another judge. Julian was quite unrepentant. He had refused to pretend that he had made up his mind. He could easily have tossed a coin to decide the matter or have said (untruthfully) that he was satisfied that one side or the other was the more accurate in their recollection. But the case made him feel more strongly than ever that it was absurd that judges should seek to try cases where the truth was so evasive. National insurance, in his view, should replace the hit-and-miss methods of purporting to ascertain liability. But in cases such as the one in which he was employing PM, whatever philosophers might say about the matter, he had no doubt that for everyday purposes the truth existed and could be ascertained. Either Mr Broad's toe had been run over by the defendant or it had not. He had been disappointed but not surprised when PM reported the result of his call upon the solicitors. But as a collector of truth he profoundly hoped that PM's further researches would prove successful.

For a moment or two he toyed with the idea of a television programme on the truth, with someone who would be the equivalent of Arthur Negus commenting upon the examples paraded before viewers.

'Here is a fine example of a half-truth. Note the way that on first examination it appears to carry complete conviction. But when you turn it upside down you will see that it is not a genuine piece. It's quite a good example and may become more valuable in time. At the moment it's only worth about ten pounds.'

Meanwhile, PM had already made his plans for getting in touch with Loudwater. He called at his house three times before he found him in.

'I'm so sorry to trouble you,' he said, 'but do you happen to be interested in racing?' He knew that he was because he'd seen him walk into a betting shop.

'Why?' asked Loudwater.

'Because I've got a system which might interest you and I'm prepared to give you a trial without obligation.'

'Why have you come to me?'

'A pure matter of chance. I'm going to about one in every ten houses here and just happened to light on you.'

'What's the proposal?'

'It's quite simple,' said PM. 'I've got a very good source of information but unfortunately I haven't the funds to do the backing.'

'That's an old story,' said Loudwater.

'To be perfectly frank with you, it is,' said PM. 'But it happens to be true on this occasion. And I can prove it to you.'

'How?'

'Well, I expect to get the winner of the 2.30 tomorrow at Birmingham. I've got a credit account with a bookmaker and if you promise to give me fifty pence if I tell you it loses, I'll bring the winnings round when it's won.'

'*If* it wins,' said Loudwater.

'Of course there's always an element of uncertainty. It might fall. The jockey might be taken ill in the middle of the race. Subject to that, I think you'll find that I shall have made you a little money. What about it?'

'You don't want any money now?' said Loudwater.

'Not a penny, and, if I do ask you for it, you're not bound to pay me, as you know. I've simply got to trust you and there's nothing I can do about it if you refuse to pay. So you can see I must have pretty good confidence in my source of information or I wouldn't take a chance on it.'

'All right. I'll give it a try,' said Loudwater. 'Fifty pence, did you say?'

'That's right.'

'OK. The 2.30 at Birmingham, you said? Can you give me any idea of what the horse is?'

'Afraid not,' said PM. 'For one thing I don't know for certain. For another, I have to keep the information absolutely confidential.'

'All right,' said Loudwater. 'I'll take a chance.'

'OK then. I'll be round at six o'clock tomorrow.'

Punctually at six o'clock the next day PM called on Loudwater and presented him with two pounds. 'Centurion at 4 to 1,' he said.

'Thank you very much,' said Loudwater. 'How much did you make for yourself?'

'That's my business, I'm afraid,' said PM. 'As long as you get your winnings, I take it you're satisfied.'

'Very satisfied. When's the next?'

'Saturday.'

'All right, I'll make it a pound this time.'

'Sorry,' said PM, 'I can't do more than fifty pence on these trial runs. It's for the three o'clock on Saturday. At Doncaster. I tell you what. Meet me in the Brewer's Arms at half past six and I'll give you your winnings there. You can buy me a drink out of them, if you like.'

At half past six in the Brewer's Arms PM handed over to Loudwater four pounds and Loudwater ordered the first drink. PM ordered the second, and the loosening-up process had begun.

PM's method of getting information from people was based largely on the two best known human failings of greed and vanity. The idea of getting something for nothing will induce many people to act. The satisfaction of personal vanity will induce many people to speak. What he proposed to do with Loudwater was at a convenient moment during their drinking to introduce the subject of the law. From the law it is easy enough to get to judges. He would then start to praise English judges and eventually he would say that he had no doubt that every judge on the Bench could tell whether a person was speaking the truth or not. He felt reasonably sure that a man like Loudwater would find it difficult not to boast about his having deceived a judge. He wouldn't come out with the whole story. That was too much to hope for. But, if you have sold a valueless painting to a picture dealer for a very large sum, you would be a very exceptional person if you did not mention this fact when the subject of selling things to experts arose. So, if Loudwater had told lie after lie to a judge and had been believed, it would be very difficult for him to resist saying at least something to show how clever he had been. PM began after the third drink.

'D'you think they'll bring back the death penalty?' he said. 'With all this violence around it might do some good, don't you think?'

'I don't much care one way or the other,' said Loudwater.

'I shouldn't like to have to pronounce it if I were a judge,' said PM.

'I shouldn't mind,' said Loudwater. 'Somebody's got to do the dirty work.'

'Yes,' said PM, 'but it's one thing to send a man to prison for a long time. If you make a mistake he can always be let out, but, if you send him away to be hanged and they hang him, you can't undo that. I wonder how many innocent men they've hanged.'

'I've never thought about it much,' said Loudwater. 'It's mostly husbands and wives who kill each other, isn't it? I expect there are a good many who've got away with it.'

'That doesn't make up for the ones who've been hanged when they shouldn't have been, but I doubt if there are many of those this century. The law's pretty good on the whole, I should say. Juries make mistakes from time to time, but I've a lot of confidence in our judges.'

Mr Loudwater did not comment on this statement.

'Yes,' went on PM. 'To tell you the truth I'd much prefer to be tried by a judge than by a jury. After all a jury consists of chaps like us and they go wrong.'

'Do you mean,' said Loudwater, 'that, if you were guilty, you would prefer to be tried by a judge or if you were innocent?'

'Oh, if I were innocent,' said PM. 'To tell you the truth, I'd prefer not to be tried at all if I were guilty. But I've read a lot about these judges and I've been to court quite often, as a matter of fact. The way they get at the truth is simply fantastic. I bet you anything you like that, if a witness is telling lies, the judge will spot it.'

Mr Loudwater said nothing.

'I've seen a witness,' went on PM, 'telling a story which seemed to me to be completely true. He was cross-examined by counsel on the other side and he stuck to his story. At the end the judge asked him three questions which showed that he'd been lying all the time.'

Mr Loudwater still said nothing.

'I don't believe it's possible for a man to go into court and swear a thing's black when he knows it's white without the judge finding out the truth.' He paused but he had to wait ten seconds before Loudwater spoke.

'What will you have?' he asked.

'Same again,' said PM. But he was not very happy about Loudwater's silence. When he came back with the drinks, PM dropped the subject for the moment, but he returned to it five or ten minutes later.

'As I was saying,' he said, 'I don't believe that the best liar in the world could put it across one of our English judges.'

Mr Loudwater opened his mouth as though he were going to say something and then he shut it again.

'You were going to say?' said PM.

'I forget,' said Mr Loudwater.

'Have you ever been in court yourself?' asked PM.

'No – yes, I have – just once.'

'Interesting?' asked PM.

'Just an accident I saw.'

'What sort of a court was it?'

'A County Court. I'd given my name to a man who was hurt and he called me as a witness. Nothing in it really.'

'Did your man win?'

'Oh yes. He couldn't help it.'

'What had happened?'

'A car had run over his foot.'

'What did it feel like giving evidence?'

'All right. After all, it was nothing to do with me, so I didn't mind what the result was.'

'Lucky for the man who was injured that you were around or he wouldn't have had a witness.'

'I suppose it was really.'

'How did the chap try to get out of it? What did he say? That the other fellow ran into the road?'

'Actually he said it didn't happen.'

'Didn't happen?' asked PM incredulously. 'I don't understand.'

'Well, he mightn't have noticed it,' said Loudwater. 'After all, he only went over a chap's foot and the light wasn't all that good.'

'But did he say that he hadn't gone over the foot?'

'Oh yes.'

'But the judge didn't believe him?'

'That's right.'

'Well, I told you, judges always get it right.'

'It was two to one,' said Loudwater.

'He hadn't got a passenger then?'

'No. Anyway, I never see anything when I'm a passenger.'

'Forgive my asking, but do you get a fee for giving evidence?'

'Oh yes. I got three pounds and my expenses, I think.'

'That isn't much for a day's work. Did your chap get damages?'

'Oh yes. Four hundred pounds.'

'He ought to have given a bit to you.'

'Well, he didn't,' said Loudwater.

PM then thought it advisable to change the subject and they went back to racing. After they'd spent half an hour on that subject PM tried once more to get Mr Loudwater to rise to the bait, but the fish wouldn't take it. The next day PM went to see Julian rather despondently.

'I'm afraid I've not had much success,' he said. 'I've brought you a recording of the interview but I'm afraid it won't help much. I must say I found it very odd that he didn't bite. After all, if we're right, he deceived a judge good and proper and here was I saying that they never were deceived. And he said nothing. I thought he was going to once but he didn't.'

'Well, let's hear it anyway,' said Julian, and they played the recording through.

'Let's have it again,' said Julian. About two-thirds of the way he stopped the tape at the point where PM had asked, 'Have you ever been in court yourself?' and Loudwater had said, 'No – yes, I have – just once.' The judge played it again. 'Have you ever been in court yourself?' 'No – yes, I have – just once.'

'That's it,' said the judge. 'That's the piece I've been looking for. How could a man who had only been in court once in his life a very short time before your interview have forgotten it? He couldn't have. Then why should he say "No"? Can you think of any reason? Unless it was that his natural instinct was not to want to refer to the subject. Now, if his natural instinct was not to want to refer to the subject, why should that be if he told the truth at the time? He was only a witness. He wasn't even a party. He'd simply gone there out of public spirit, you might say, to back up a genuine claim. And yet when he's asked if he's ever been in court he at first says "No". I know he corrected it at once but I can't think of any honest reason for his saying it at all. That's the one answer that doesn't fit into the jigsaw puzzle and that means that Loudwater's in the fraud.'

'Why didn't he say something,' said PM, 'when I tempted him? He might at least have said something when I said that judges could always find out the truth or words to that effect – he might at least have said "That's all you know" or something like that. He didn't have to come out with the whole story. And if he was telling lies in the witness box, it must have been a great effort of self-control on his part not to contradict me in some way. He didn't even say, "Really?" with a knowing smile. He did absolutely nothing to show that he'd scored off a judge. That isn't human nature.'

'It's human nature to defend yourself,' said Julian. 'It's human nature not to admit that you've committed a crime. Indeed, that was why he started off by saying "No". His first instinct, you see, was to protect himself, by denying the incident altogether. Then he quickly remembered that it didn't hurt him to say that he'd been to a court and it was probably better to admit it. I quite agree that your ploy is a good one and often it will have some result, but it is not bound to do so. It's perfectly true that there are quite a number of murderers who've given themselves away simply out of vanity but there must be a large number – a larger number I should say – who have not. After all, deliberately to give oneself away is a very stupid thing to do and contrary to one's natural instincts. So there's a natural instinct of self-preservation fighting against the natural instinct of vanity, and in Loudwater's case self-preservation came first. Indeed, there was too much self-preservation in his case. He said "No" when you asked him if he'd ever been to court before and that was an instinctive "No" which he couldn't check. It was like the man who's charged with stealing from cars and therefore doesn't like to admit that he was in the street where the cars were; or the shoplifter who prefers not to admit that he's been in the particular department from which he'd taken the things. Oh no, you've done very well, Mr Mountjoy,' said Julian. 'And I'm very pleased. We've got over our first hurdle. You've established to my satisfaction that Loudwater was a party to the fraud. The question is what do we do now? What do you usually do when you've found out that the man you're following is guilty but that you haven't any evidence to prove it? How do you set about getting the evidence?'

'It all depends on the case,' said PM. 'To tell you the truth I haven't the faintest idea what I shall do next. I might prove an association between him and the plaintiff.'

'There may not be one,' said Julian. 'If, as I believe, this is part of a much bigger racket, that little episode has been cleared up, the parties have had their profit and Loudwater may never come into the picture again. Of course it's possible he will. If they liked the way he gave his evidence they might use him again, but that's rather dangerous. I think you've probably got to – ' and then Julian broke off and thought for a few minutes. Finally he said: 'I think it should be fairly plain sailing from now on.'

'Who's going to do the sailing?' asked PM.

'Both of us, I think,' said Julian.

'Well, I'm glad to know there's to be no problem about it, but, to be perfectly honest, I wouldn't know what to do.'

'I'm not saying that you ought to have known,' said Julian, 'but, if the truth is what I believe it to be and we act logically on the basis that it is the truth, we are almost bound to achieve what we want.'

'You ought to be in the business, if I may say so,' said PM.

'I appear to be at the moment,' said Julian. 'I must admit that I find it rather exhilarating. I believe that one judge said that the stern chase after a lie which has got the start is apt to be a long one, and C H Spurgeon said, "A lie travels round the world while truth is putting on her boots." There's a good deal in both these statements, but I think that this time, thanks to you, truth has got her boots on and all we need to do is to keep them moving while the scent is still good. Can you change your voice if you want to?'

'Wotcha mean?' said PM.

'No, I don't mean that,' said Julian. 'A higher or lower tone – different from your own voice.'

'To be perfectly honest,' said PM, 'I'm not all that good at it, but I can try,' he added, in a deep bass.

'Too obvious.'

'How's that?' asked PM in a high treble.

'Not much better.' Julian thought for a moment. 'I may have to do it myself.'

'Might I ask what?'

'Have you got your friend's telephone number?'

'Loudwater's, d'you mean?'

'Yes, of course.'

'He's in the telephone book, as a matter of fact. Are you going to ring him up?'

'I'd have preferred you to, but I don't want to risk his recognising your voice.'

'What are you going to say to him?'

'You'll see,' said Julian. 'Put a new tape in your tape-recorder and fix it so that it will pick up both sides of this telephone interview.'

'If I may say so,' said PM, 'you seem very confident that your plan will succeed.'

'I am,' said Julian. 'If you follow the truth logically everything must fall into place. Of course, if our premise is wrong, we shall fail. But then we ought to fail, because the truth won't be what we think it is. But don't forget that I heard the evidence in this case and I don't believe the defendant can be wrong. And when we find that the man who gave evidence that he saw him swerve into and out of Shallow Place at first denied that he had ever given evidence before, that fact makes it almost certain that my intuition was correct. I cannot conceive how an ordinary, honest man could at first have said "No" when he was asked if he's ever been in court. It was only for a moment,

I agree, but that's what I would expect. For a split second he couldn't control the defensive mechanism in his mind. This said to him that by admitting that he'd given evidence in court he was admitting that he'd committed a crime, so he said "No". In the very unlikely event of my being wrong about that, I'll be shown to be wrong altogether. In any event the truth is either that he was completely honest and did see the accident or that he was paid to give false evidence. Until I was as sure as I could be that it was in fact a conspiracy I didn't want to put it to the test, but, now that I am so sure, I'm going to do so. And one way or the other the truth will emerge. Now fix up your tape recorder, please, and then get the number. Don't say anything yourself, but leave it to me.'

A few minutes later Loudwater answered the telephone and Julian spoke to him. 'You won't know me,' he said, 'but could I have a word with you?'

'Who is it?' asked Loudwater.

'Never mind that for the moment,' said Julian. 'This is confidential. A little while ago you did a job for us.'

'What d'you mean? A job?' asked Loudwater.

'At Hambrook County Court.'

Loudwater said nothing.

'Are you there?' asked Julian.

'Yes,' said Loudwater.

Julian waited a full ten seconds for Loudwater to say something more, but he didn't say anything. Julian was now thoroughly satisfied that he was right. A person who was completely innocent in the matter and had simply given evidence about an accident which he happened to have seen would have been bound to ask what it was all about, but Loudwater said nothing. After the silence, Julian went on, 'We want to know if you'll do another one for us?'

'Another one?' queried Loudwater.

'Yes,' said Julian. 'It will be worth twice as much to you.'

Again Loudwater said nothing.

'It's much easier than last time. We shall only want you to say that you took the number of the car, not that you saw the accident.'

'In advance?' said Loudwater.

'How d'you mean?' said Julian.

'Payment.'

'Oh no,' said Julian, 'you can have it after the case is over.'

'But supposing it went wrong? Would I have it just the same?'

'It won't. It can't.'

'Let me have half in advance,' said Loudwater.

'Twenty-five pounds, if you like,' said Julian.

'All right. When will you tell me all about it?'

'The chap who fixed it with you last time will come and see you or fix a meeting somewhere else. All right with you?'

'OK,' said Loudwater.

'Goodbye then,' said Julian.

'Goodbye.'

And the conversation ended.

'Play that back, please,' said Julian. 'Just to see that it's been recorded properly.'

PM did so and the conversation could be plainly heard.

'Well I'm blessed,' said PM. 'Why were you so sure it would come off?'

'I was only sure it would come off if he was in the swindle,' said Julian. 'Put yourself in his position. He *was* in the swindle. What else could he have said? From his point of view he was speaking to a man who knew in fact that he'd given false evidence. What was the good of his pretending that he hadn't? Secondly, he could sense that he was going to make some more money, so that, if he was part of the racket, even on the fringe, he was bound to say something incriminating. The poor chap couldn't help it. Even his silence was incriminating. An innocent man would have been bound to say something like "I don't know what you're talking about. What on earth is this?" and so on. Not so Mr Loudwater.'

'How much d'you think he'll get?' said PM.

'Loudwater, d'you mean?' said Julian.

'Yes.'

'Nothing at all, if I have my way. He's the man who can help us to crack the conspiracy wide open and that's what he's going to have to do. Fortunately, as far as we know, he's a man of good character. That's to say, he's got no convictions against him. If he were an old hand, it would have been much more difficult because they're frightened of retaliation if they give other people away and also there is a code among confirmed criminals. Look at the train robbers. None of them has given the slightest indication where the money went. If one of them had spilt the beans he would certainly have got substantial remission and he still would. But not a word from any of them. With any luck Mr Loudwater is not in the same category and he'll talk and help. I grant you there's the possibility that he won't, in which case the answer to your question would, I should think, be two years, possibly more.'

'What are we going to do now?'

'Now?' said Julian. 'We shall set the steam-roller moving. I'll make an appointment with the Commissioner at Scotland Yard and you can come with me and bring your tape-recorder.'

The same afternoon Julian and PM were interviewed by the Commissioner and a superintendent of the CID. Julian explained what had happened.

'I believe,' he went on, 'that we shall unearth a conspiracy up and down the country to put forward comparatively small claims and to use somewhat seedy but unconvicted people to back them up.'

'May I ask why you were so sure you'd get the evidence?' asked the Commissioner. 'As far as I can see it was based on one word only – "No".'

'That's right,' said Julian. 'But if it hadn't been "No" it would have been something else. If you ask enough questions and record all the questions and answers, one answer will eventually show that the truth is not being told, *if* it is not being told.'

'Well,' said the Commissioner, 'what do you suggest that we should do now?'

'That's a matter for you, Commissioner, but, if you want my view on the matter, I suggest that the superintendent comes down with another officer and Mr Mountjoy and me and we interview Mr Loudwater to give him the opportunity of assisting us or going to prison. I think you will find he will assist us, certainly if we're right in thinking that he's got no previous convictions.'

'Very well,' said the Commissioner, 'I suggest the superintendent goes down with you this evening. In my view the evening is always the best time to make a man talk. He's enjoying himself looking at television and thinking of a happy night in bed and he's suddenly faced with a complete upheaval of his life. Even old hands don't like it, but for a chap who's never been inside it must be hell. I agree with you, I think he'll talk.'

The same evening Julian and PM, accompanied by the superintendent and a detective-inspector and two detective-constables, called on Loudwater.

When he opened the door to them the superintendent told him who he was and said he wanted to interview him.

'What about?' asked Loudwater.

'May we come inside?' asked the superintendent. 'Then we'll tell you.'

Loudwater let them in, but the two detective-constables remained outside. Their duty was to follow Loudwater wherever he went, if he were not arrested. When they'd all sat down in Loudwater's sitting-room, the superintendent began.

'We want to play you a tape-recording,' he said, and he played over the telephone conversation between Loudwater and Julian. Loudwater said nothing at the end but his face had lost some colour.

'Now,' said the superintendent, 'you recognise your own voice?'

As Loudwater didn't reply, he said: 'Do you recognise your own voice, Mr Loudwater?'

'No.'

'Well, it sounds different to you if you've not heard it before on tape but the other voice was that of this gentleman here,' and he indicated Julian. 'This gentleman is in fact a retired judge,' he added, 'and was present throughout the trial to which that conversation was referring. He heard all your evidence and he is as satisfied as I am that it was completely false and that you'd been paid to give that evidence.'

'Can you prove that?' said Loudwater, without very much conviction.

'This tape-recording proves it,' said the superintendent. 'But whether we prove it in court or not is up to you. At least, whether we prove it against you is a matter for you.'

'Can I see a solicitor?' asked Loudwater.

'Not at the moment,' said the superintendent. 'The position is this. In my opinion we've got ample evidence against you to put you in the dock and charge you with conspiracy with people unknown. In that case you'll either plead guilty or you'll plead not guilty and the judge will tell you how much he thinks you'll get, if you want to know, but I can tell you that it'll be a very long time. That's one alternative. Do you understand?'

'I suppose so,' said Loudwater.

'The other alternative,' said the superintendent, 'is that you assist us to find out who is in this swindle.'

'I don't know,' said Loudwater. 'Really, I don't.'

'That's rubbish,' said the superintendent. 'You know that Broad is in it.'

'Apart from him,' said Loudwater.

'But *he* wasn't the man who approached you,' said the superintendent.

'I don't know who he is,' said Loudwater.

'How did he get in touch with you?'

'He met me coming away from work.'

'What happened? I should tell you that the inspector's recording this conversation.'

'Well, we went and had a drink at the pub and after we'd had a few he asked me whether I'd like to earn a little money on the side. I asked him how and then he told me. D'you promise that if I go on and tell you everything, you won't prosecute me?'

'If what you tell us is true,' said the superintendent, 'we won't. If you tell us one lie, we will.'

'I might make a mistake.'

'Well don't,' said the superintendent. 'You'll find it expensive. We want the truth – and no mistake. Now you admit that you never saw the accident and that this man who took you to the pub told you that you'd be required to give evidence that you had seen it and that's in fact what you did?'

'Yes,' said Loudwater.

'Did you meet anybody else before the trial?'

'Yes. Mr Broad.'

'Anyone else?'

'No.'

'How much were you paid?'

'Thirty-five pounds.'

'In cash, I suppose?'

'Yes.'

'Who gave you the money?'

'The chap who took me to the pub.'

'Is this the only time you've done it?'

'Yes. I'd be prepared to swear to that.'

'Well, I believe you,' said Julian, 'in spite of the fact that you're prepared to swear to it.'

'What d'you want me to do?' asked Loudwater.

'Quite a lot,' said the superintendent. 'When we've finished here we're going along to Mr Broad and in front of him you'll tell me all you've told us today and any more that comes into your head, provided it's true.'

'You'll give me police protection?'

'We'll give you all you need,' said the superintendent, 'provided you play ball with us. And if you don't, prison will give you all the protection you need.'

Later that evening the party called on Broad.

'Now, Mr Broad,' said the superintendent, when he'd introduced everyone to him, 'the position is this. You brought a fraudulent action against Mr Crane and you're going to be charged with perjury and conspiracy and I warn you that anything you now say will be used in evidence when you're prosecuted. But I'm going to give you an opportunity to say anything if you wish to do so. Mr Loudwater has admitted that he was procured to give false evidence in your favour and that he did so. Now, there are two ways you can go about this and it's up to you which you do. You can have the opportunity of seeing your solicitor, if you want, before you decide what you're going to do. It's quite obvious that there's a big conspiracy to obtain money by fraud and perjury. If you help us to unearth that conspiracy you will still be prosecuted but we will certainly say to the judge, when it comes to the question of sentence, that you've helped us all you can, if you do help us all you can. So it's up to you to make up your mind. If you want to go into another room and think about it by all means do so. It's probably too late for you to get on to a solicitor, but you can do so in the morning if you want to, before you give us any answer. I shan't charge you formally till after you've seen your solicitor, but don't try to run away or do anything silly like that. You won't be successful and it will only go against you. And I warn you that you'll be under observation from now onwards.'

Broad thought for a bit. 'I'm glad you've come,' he said eventually, 'it's been on my conscience. I've never done anything like this before, but it seemed too easy. I'll give you all the help I can.'

'Good,' said the superintendent. 'If you keep to that, we won't oppose bail and we'll do all we can to get you off with a light sentence. If it's true that this is the first time you've ever done it, we shall be much more interested to get the people who are running the racket than we are to get you. Now, would you like to make a statement?'

'Yes, I would. And I'll tell you the truth.'

'The whole truth and nothing but the truth?' said the superintendent.

'Yes.'

'You swore to do that in the court,' said the superintendent. 'How are we to know that what you say this time will be any more truthful than what you said in court?'

'For one thing,' said Broad, with a sort of smile, 'I'm not being paid to say what I'm going to say now.'

'That's a good point,' said the superintendent. 'Well, take a deep breath and tell me all you know and the inspector will take it down.'

Eventually, with the assistance of Broad and Loudwater and by following up all the information which they gave, the police were able to discover that the whole conspiracy had been engineered by a clerk in a solicitor's office who, unknown to the solicitor, had a previous record for fraud. Some of the cases were put through his own firm but he made sure that there were not too many to excite the suspicions of the insurance company. He used to go all round the country in his spare time fixing up cases and then sending the people concerned to respectable solicitors and telling them what to say. Having regard to his experience in a solicitor's office he knew pretty well exactly how to brief everyone engaged in the swindle. It transpired that over two hundred claims had been made and only seventy-five of these had ever come to court. The insurance companies had settled the others. From their point of view the chances of success in defending the actions were too small to justify a fight, particularly when the plaintiff was prepared to accept a reasonable amount in discharge of liability. The ringleader was very careful to see that the damages were never exaggerated. No false claims for special damage were ever put forward. Any claim for actual out-of-pocket expenses could be proved up to the hilt. And no very serious claims were ever brought. His motto was 'little and often'. He too, like PM, relied upon the greed of people to get something for nothing. He found out people with recent injuries who were prepared to lend themselves to the fraud. Occasionally when somebody had some slight scruples about it, he brushed these scruples aside successfully by pointing out that it was only an insurance company that would have to pay. Unfortunately there are many people who don't think anything of cheating the Government, insurance companies, or indeed, any large concern. Of course it took rather more nerve to go into the witness box and swear to things which had never happened, but there the incentive of getting a substantial sum for nothing was a sufficient attraction to those who agreed to the scheme. After the prosecution was all over, Julian lunched with the Commissioner. After lunch the Commissioner offered him a cigar.

'No, thank you,' said Julian.

'Have you ever smoked?' asked the Commissioner.

'No,' said Julian, 'well, yes, I did once for a very short time.'

'No – yes?' said the Commissioner. And they both smiled.

CHAPTER FIVE

Poison-Pen

Some weeks after the accident conspiracy had been disposed of the Commissioner telephoned to Julian and asked whether he might send a superintendent to see him.

'What have I done now?' asked Julian.

'I'd like to send down Superintendent Carson with the shorthand note of a case which is worrying me rather. I'd prefer not to talk about it on the telephone but would you mind seeing him and then, if you can spare the time to read through the shorthand note, give me your opinion about it? The superintendent will explain everything.'

'Certainly,' said Julian. He was extremely pleased at the idea of having to investigate another case and the fact that the Commissioner was consulting him showed that he hadn't trodden on any police corns in his previous investigation. Julian had a high opinion of the police but at the same time realised that the Force, like every other institution, had its deficiencies. From his experience of the cases in which he'd appeared as counsel or which he'd tried and from his conversations with other judges and with lawyers, he felt reasonably certain that the great majority of policemen were people of integrity. But what they lacked on the whole was brain-power. In the 1970s a much higher standard of intelligence was required than ever before. In Julian's view there ought to be a new recruiting policy for the police. Young men and women of good character and physique and of high intelligence should be encouraged to join, but, human nature being what it is, it is difficult to encourage such young men and women to join a profession where the rewards are much less than in other professions which are open to them. Julian would have liked to see the present pay of the police doubled and the standard of entry made much more difficult. The police should compete for candidates with the Bar, solicitors, accountants, surveyors and businesses of all kinds. At the moment it was under strength in brains as well as in numbers, and he regretted that no Government since the war had had the courage to do what was essential if the streets and homes in England were to remain safe for people to walk in and live in.

He awaited the arrival of Superintendent Carson with some eagerness. He had been very pleased at putting right the injustice in the accident case and bringing to justice the criminals responsible for it. But one such experience was not enough and it occurred to him that he was welcoming the possibility of a second experience almost as a young barrister welcomes his second brief. As one grows older it is noticeable that time goes much faster. A child, told that he must rest for an hour or that something will not happen for an hour, feels that he has got to wait almost for eternity. Normally for an adult an hour goes all too quickly. But on this occasion Julian found himself looking at his watch almost every five minutes, and he was really delighted when at last there was a ring at the bell and the superintendent arrived.

He took him into his study and offered him a drink, which the superintendent refused. It was not a question of being on duty, he explained. 'Even one glass of sherry makes me slower in concentrating.'

'Well,' said Julian, helping himself, 'I hope you'll forgive me. I can't say it makes me any quicker but I certainly haven't noticed any slowing-down process. Now please sit down and make yourself at home and tell me what it's all about.'

'It's a long story,' said the superintendent, 'and a rather odd one. You've probably read a certain amount about it but the Press hasn't got room to print half the evidence in these cases. It's that recent poison-pen letters case.'

'The parson at Pendlebury, you mean?' asked Julian.

'That's right. As you know, he's been convicted and his appeal's been dismissed.'

'Then the Commissioner's not happy about it?' asked Julian. 'Or is it you? I take it that you were in charge of the case?'

'Yes,' said the superintendent, 'I was. As a matter of fact, neither of us is very happy about it.'

'Perhaps you'd remind me of the main facts.'

'I will. Pendlebury is a village in Kent and there are about two or three thousand people living in the neighbourhood. The Reverend Walter Kingsdown is the parson. He's been there for ten years.'

'Is he married?' said Julian.

'Yes. Married and apparently very happily married. That is one of the odd things about the case. Usually when you find a parson doing this sort of thing there's some history of eccentric behaviour or trouble at home. There's nothing of the sort in this case. He appears to be a normal and intelligent man and popular in the neighbourhood. About six months before the trial these letters started to arrive. They were nasty sort of letters and the worst part about them was that they appeared to be based on some kind of truth. They were mostly concerned with domestic scandals, adultery, cruelty and obscenity, and very few of the allegations appeared to be absolutely without foundation.'

'How many letters were there altogether?'

'Of course we can't be certain about that, because some people may have preferred not to bring them to the police, but the charges were in respect of sixteen letters.'

'What was the worst?'

'I suppose the worst was the one which alleged that Colonel Highweek had murdered his wife. I say it was the worst because it might well have been true. I don't know what your feelings are, your Honour, but I'm afraid I was all on the side of the colonel. I should probably have done much the same myself. His wife was dying and in considerable pain but likely to live for a long time. The coroner, in my view quite rightly, didn't probe too much into the matter and a verdict of accidental death was returned. The colonel was, I'm sure, devoted to his wife and that's why I think that that letter was the worst of the lot. Most of the others were the usual sort of thing about husbands playing about with other women and occasionally wives playing about with other men. There was one allegation of shoplifting – I can't think for a moment that there was any truth in it.'

'A man or a woman?' asked Julian.

'A woman. A most respectable person and in no financial trouble.'

'I'm afraid that financial trouble often has little to do with shoplifting,' said Julian. 'But whether or not there's any substance in the allegation is only relevant in so far as it may shed a little light on the person who made it.'

'Exactly,' said the superintendent.

'Why should a parson, popular in the neighbourhood and happily married, do things like this?'

'That's the question we asked ourselves and of course we at first thought that it might be his wife.'

'Then you had a doubt as to which of them it was?' asked Julian, but before the superintendent could reply, he went on: 'I'm sorry. I shouldn't keep interrupting you. Tell me the whole story. What was the evidence against him?'

'Quite simply,' said the superintendent, 'that all these letters were typed on the same typewriter and that typewriter belongs to Mr Kingsdown.'

'So either he or his wife could have used it?'

'Yes, or I suppose they could have done it together. I've never heard of such a case,' said the superintendent, 'but I suppose it's possible.'

'Have they any children?'

'No.'

'Does anyone else live in the house?'

'No.'

'Have they any daily help?'

'Yes, they have, but we went into that most carefully. It's quite plain that Mrs Stoker, who comes in two or three times a week, would have been quite incapable of writing these letters. Even if she could have typed them out, which is most improbable, the letters are grammatically correct and the spelling is excellent.'

'Do they have anybody to stay with them?'

'Occasionally but very rarely, and we've been able to eliminate the only two people who stayed with them during the period in question.'

'How did the matter first come to your attention?'

'A Mr and Mrs Truman took a letter to the police. They'd in fact had some domestic difficulties but they'd got over them. The letter in question showed that the writer knew a good deal about them and they brought it to the police straightaway and asked the local CID to try to find out who'd done it. The letter was entirely typewritten and was signed "An Ill-wisher".

'Perhaps I'd better see it, as it's the first of them.'

'Certainly,' and the superintendent produced a copy. It read as follows:

> The Seat of Knowledge,
> Pendlebury, Kent.
> 16th March.

Dear Mr and Mrs Truman,

Don't you think it's about time you came to church again? You may think that you can successfully hush up your sins from man but you certainly cannot do so from God. There is little to choose between either of you. You, Mr Truman, committed adultery and you, Mrs Truman, winked at it, connived is the legal word, I believe. That, to my mind, is just as bad. You swore in church to be faithful to each other. You promised your Maker that you would forsake all others and devote yourselves entirely to each other. Within seven years you have broken that promise and I can only imagine that you, Mrs Truman, winked at your husband's adultery because you had your own plans for yourself. I don't say it was the milkman or the postman, because I think you're a little more discriminating than that, but I don't know why a rather good-looking young man should seek unsuccessfully to sell you a colour television set and should call on you for this purpose no less than four times. Mr Truman, were you aware of this? God was if you were not. If you wish to avoid the consequences of your sins, you will come to church each week and put a pound in the collection instead of your usual 10 pence. If you do what I tell you, I will reconsider your case after a year. Mind you, I make no promises – except this. If you don't do what I tell you, I will make your life a hell and you will indeed have a foretaste of what is to come hereafter.

Yours most sincerely,

AN ILL-WISHER.

'And that was typed on the parson's typewriter?'

'It was.'

'There's no doubt about that at all, I imagine? The test was a hundred percent, I assume?'

'It was, and Mr Kingsdown agreed that it must have been typed on his typewriter.'

'But I presume he denied that either he or his wife had typed it.'

'He did.'

'And when did the next letter arrive?'

'The next one was a similar one but instead of saying that they must put a pound in the collection at church it said that they must enter into a covenant with a charity.'

'Presumably you investigated the charity?'

'Of course. There are only three or four people who really run it. None of them has even been to Pendlebury, let alone to the vicarage.'

'But I'd be right in thinking,' asked Julian, 'that the writer of the letters – all or most of them – writes in a semi-religious way but warns the people concerned that they must do what the writer says if they don't want to get into further trouble?'

'That is substantially correct.'

'So in effect all the letters are the sort of letters which an unbalanced parson might have written?'

'Exactly.'

'Are they all told that they've got to go to church regularly?'

'Most of them, but some of them are given other penances such as offering to help at the cottage hospital, offering to become a prison visitor in the nearest jail, which by the way is twenty-five miles away.'

'It appears fairly clear that the writer has a sort of power complex. He or she wants to get pleasure from making people do the things that they're told to do. If I'm right in thinking that, I assume that the majority of the letters require them to go to church.'

'Correct.'

'So that he or she could have the pleasure of watching people, who don't often go there, going as often as they've been told.'

'I quite agree.'

'When did you first ask the parson questions about the letters?'

'Oh, I didn't go myself. The local inspector went. He really went for help. Nobody suspected the parson at first, but the inspector asked Mr Kingsdown if he could think of anybody who it might have been, anybody who was a little deranged or on the way to being a religious maniac or anything of that sort.'

'Could he make any suggestions?'

'He mentioned a Mrs Wallet who at times had thought that she was the Virgin Mary. She was otherwise quite harmless and there was nothing to connect her with the letters.'

'I meant to ask you this before. Did the parson or his wife ever have any letters themselves?'

'I'm coming to that. The last one of all was to him.'

'I'd better see it.'

The superintendent produced a copy and it read as follows:

> The Seat of Knowledge,
> Pendlebury, Kent.
> 19th September.

Dear Vicar,

Woe to you, you hypocrite. How can you get up in the pulpit each Sunday and preach the doctrine of brotherly love? You should be ashamed of yourself. God is watching you, I tell you. And so am I. How many of your parishioners have you visited in the last month? I don't pretend you're overpaid. Very few parsons are. But you shouldn't have taken the job if you weren't prepared to give full value for the money you receive. From the first of next month I shall expect you to visit at least twenty people a day. I shall also expect you to preach sermons of exactly twelve and a half minutes, timed by your watch and by mine. And there are other things that go on at the vicarage of which I am aware but of which the ecclesiastical authorities are not yet aware. If you don't do what I tell you, they will become aware of these goings-on. You may think that when you shut the door and draw the blinds no one can tell what you're doing. Not even God. But you are wrong. Be sure your sins will find you out. I shall not warn you again.

> Yours most sincerely,
>
> AN ILL-WISHER.

'And that was on the same typewriter?'

'Yes,' said the superintendent.

'Were there any goings-on behind the blinds?'

'The vicar said that occasionally, when they had a party of young people, they played sardines.'

'St Paul said nothing against that as far as I can remember,' said Julian. 'Well, what happened?'

'The inspector went back to see the vicar about a fortnight later. He then asked him if he had a typewriter. The vicar said that he had. "D'you mind if I have a look at it and take a sample from it?" asked the inspector. "By all means," said the vicar. "I ought to have offered you the opportunity before, but I must admit that I didn't think I could be suspected of sending these letters myself. Anyway you're bound to find that I haven't. No two typewriters are the same." The inspector said that he wasn't suspecting the vicar for a moment – and indeed he wasn't – but that it was necessary to eliminate every typewriter in the neighbourhood if possible. No one was more surprised than the inspector when it looked even to a layman as though the letters were written on that typewriter. He and the vicar spent half an hour checking the various slight peculiarities of each letter, the spaces between them and so on. At the end the vicar readily admitted that it looked as though the letters had been typed on that typewriter. "But not by me," he said, "nor of course by my wife. I'm as horrified at these evil things as you are."

'After this had been reported to me,' went on the superintendent, 'I felt that I'd better come on the scene myself. After all, it's a terrible charge to make against a parson. It's bad enough against anyone, but a parson would be completely ruined by it. So I went down to see him myself and I asked him if he could suggest anyone who could have sent the letters. "We've been thinking about that ever since the inspector called," he said, "but we can't think of anyone. There are people in the neighbourhood who could have access to the actual information that's referred to in them" – because by that time I'd shown him various letters – "but I can't think of anyone who'd stoop to doing it. It can't be us, either, superintendent," he said. "Why do you say it *can't* be?" I asked. "Well, there's one written to us," he said. I'm afraid I said that that was quite a normal practice. "I'm not for the moment saying you have sent them," I said, "but writers of poison-pen letters often write one to themselves in the hope that it will put people off the scent." "Well, all I can say, superintendent," said the vicar, "is that neither my wife nor I wrote these letters." "You can say that for yourself, vicar," I said, "but your wife must speak for herself." "I'll ask her to come in," he said. He went out and brought in his wife and she told me that she'd had no part in writing the letters and that she was sure her husband hadn't written them either.

' "It's very difficult for us, Mr and Mrs Kingsdown," I said. "Here are all these letters, apparently typed on your typewriter, and as far as I can see there's no one else who can have typed them."

' "I know that Walter couldn't have," said Mrs Kingsdown.

' "How are you so certain?"

' "A wife knows her husband. I know he could never have done such a thing."

' "Well, I wouldn't have thought so either," I said, "but one has to face the facts."

' "What are you going to do?" asked the vicar.

' "I'll have to consider the matter, but it's a very difficult decision for me to make. Is there anything else either of you want to say?" They had nothing to add and I went away. A week later I was telephoned by Mrs Kingsdown and she asked if I'd call and see her in the absence of her husband. So of course I went. "Well, Mrs Kingsdown?" I said, when we were alone. "I'm afraid I told you an untruth," she said. "My husband knew nothing whatever about the letters. I typed them." "I hope you realise," I said, "what a serious admission you're making." "Yes, of course," she said. "Are you prepared to sign a statement to that effect?" "Yes, I am. What will happen to me?" "I can't say for certain, but you'll probably be charged with publishing criminal libels." I was just about to go when a thought suddenly occurred to me. "Oh, Mrs Kingsdown," I said, "could I look at the typewriter again?" "Certainly," she said. We went into the vicar's study and I put the typewriter on a table. "Now," I said, "Mrs Kingsdown, will you be good enough to get a piece of paper and type out a line or two." "Me?" she said. "Yes." "What do you want me to type?" "Anything you like. Perhaps you'd do the whole thing, put in the paper and so on." While she was getting the paper I put my hand behind the typewriter and locked it. In consequence she found she couldn't roll on the paper. "I've locked it," I said. "All you have to do is to unlock it – just press the little lever." She didn't know where to find it. "Mrs Kingsdown," I said, "I don't believe you know how to type, I don't believe you've ever typed anything on this typewriter in your life." She burst into tears.'

'So she believed her husband was guilty and was trying to protect him?' asked Julian.

'Naturally that's what I thought and I asked her about it. She was quite sure her husband would never do such a thing, but her trouble was to think who else could have done it. She knew she hadn't done it herself and she couldn't resist the conclusion that it was her husband in spite of the fact that it was completely out of character and she couldn't conceive him doing it. But she'd been brooding over the matter and realised that the consequences to him if he were convicted were appalling. It would ruin their whole lives, whereas if she were convicted, although it would be bad for them it wouldn't reflect upon him. And then she asked me if I believed her husband was guilty. I said quite truthfully that I didn't want to believe it but that we were being forced to that conclusion and I added that her rather foolish behaviour, although I quite understood it, harmed her husband rather than helped him. A day or two later the inspector and I interviewed the vicar and his wife. I told him what his wife had said and he replied that she did it out of a misguided sense of loyalty to him. He said she couldn't type and that she'd never used that typewriter. This provided us, I'm afraid, with a very important piece of evidence. As your Honour knows, if in a criminal prosecution you can only prove that one of two people has done something but you can't prove which, the jury is bound to acquit both. Once the vicar had admitted that his wife could not have done it and had not done it there appeared to us to be sufficient evidence to prefer a charge against him. He was accordingly charged and, as you know, eventually convicted.'

'What I want to know,' said Julian, 'is what is worrying you and the Commissioner? You wouldn't have come to me unless you had some serious doubt about the matter. All the letters were typed on the vicar's typewriter, he had the sort of knowledge which would have enabled him to write them, his wife didn't write them, and the only person who came regularly to the house, apart from them, was a woman who couldn't possibly have written them. So the inevitable conclusion is that he wrote them. The jury apparently had no doubt about it.'

'Oh, I wouldn't say that,' said the superintendent. 'They were out for three hours, so one or two of them must have had some doubts.'

'Was the verdict unanimous?'

'Yes, it was.'

'What is it that you and the Commissioner are so worried about, then?'

'I can put that quite simply. I have spoken to the vicar on a number of occasions and I've heard him give evidence and I must say that I believe he's telling the truth. There's been no prevarication by him of any kind, he's answered all our questions, and as far as I can tell from his character and past life it is almost inconceivable that he did this.'

'Stranger things have happened.' said Julian. 'People occasionally have surprised their best friends by behaving in an outrageous way.'

'I know,' said the superintendent, 'and we've had to act on the basis that that's the case here or we wouldn't have brought the charge. But the Commissioner's very worried about it and so am I, and we'd be very grateful if you'd read the whole of the report of the proceedings and, if he is prepared to give you an interview, go and see the parson for yourself in prison and try to form a view.'

'But suppose I do form the view that you and the Commissioner have taken? What can be done about it?'

'We hoped you'd tell us that.'

'Well,' said Julian, 'if there's some fresh evidence, the Home Secretary can refer the matter to the Court of Appeal for a further hearing, but I'm afraid the mere fact that I said I believed the man first of all wouldn't be admitted as evidence and secondly wouldn't be of any value if it were. The question was, did the jury believe him and they obviously didn't.'

'I quite follow all that but, knowing what you did in that accident case, the Commissioner felt it was just worthwhile asking you if you could see anything that had been overlooked before the Ecclesiastical authorities take action.'

'Why was he sent to prison?' asked Julian.

'The judge didn't want to send him,' said the superintendent, 'and asked him to give an undertaking not to send any further letters. He refused on the ground that it was tantamount to admitting that he was guilty. Although the judge tried to persuade him, he refused to budge and was sent to prison for nine months.'

'Well, I'll read the papers with pleasure, but I must confess that at the moment I can't see what I shall be able to suggest. Of course, if I come to the conclusion that there's definitely been a miscarriage of justice, I shall do all I can to suggest something to put the matter right. In fact, if I do come to that conclusion I believe that we shall be able to find something to justify the conclusion. The truth may be at the bottom of a well but, if it is, we'll let somebody down to find it. And haul him up again with it. I'm afraid on what you've told me I doubt if this will happen. Anyway I'll read the papers at once and let you know.'

CHAPTER SIX

An Angry Parson

The superintendent left and the judge immediately got down to examining the case. He found that the superintendent's summary was substantially accurate, but when he'd read the papers through twice he telephoned Scotland Yard.

'Superintendent,' he said, 'in your evidence you said that, at a time when you had no suspicion whatever of the vicar, an inspector called upon him to see whether he could give any help as to who might have written the letters.'

'That's right.'

'And that was on the 18th September last.'

'That is so.'

'Is there any possibility of that being a mistake?' asked Julian.

'None whatever. I have the inspector's notebook in front of me and it says the 18th September.'

'Will you look at the dates before and after that and see if it fits in.'

'Yes, I will, but I can see as I look at the notebook that he had another interview with someone else about a completely different matter on the same date but at a different hour, and that is after the interview with the vicar. But I'll just look and see if there was anything before the interview with him. Oh yes, I see there was. And now I see that the previous date is the 17th and the date after is the 19th so there's no possibility of there being a mistake.'

'Well then, I shall come and see you and the Commissioner at once if that's convenient.'

That afternoon Julian went to Scotland Yard and was soon with the Commissioner and the superintendent.

'Have you found something?' said the Commissioner.

'Yes,' said Julian, 'I have. Whoever wrote those letters was at pains to see that he or she was not discovered. Very common paper that could be bought anywhere was used. Everything was typed, both on the envelopes and in the letters themselves. Now the vicar's an intelligent person and it's quite plain that, if he wrote the letters, he didn't want to be found out. He has consistently denied his guilt but, as the superintendent said, he hasn't prevaricated at all and, when his wife stupidly confessed to having written the letters, he made you a present of the evidence necessary to convict him.'

'Where does that get us?' said the Commissioner.

'So far from admitting his guilt, the vicar has denied it each time without hesitation. He plainly did not want to be prosecuted or convicted.'

'We can agree about that,' said the Commissioner.

'Now it's perfectly true,' said Julian, 'that people who write these letters do sometimes write them to themselves in order to try to put people off the scent. But they don't send them in their own handwriting and sign them.'

'I don't follow,' said the Commissioner. 'None of the letters was handwritten.'

'The one that was written to the vicar identified the writer as clearly as if it had been written by him. And it was written on the day *after* the inspector's visit.'

'A typewriter isn't quite the same thing,' said the Commissioner.

'It can prove even more plainly than handwriting that a letter emanates from a particular household. Handwriting may be a matter of argument. A handwriting expert may be wrong. But where you find that all the idiosyncrasies of a particular typewriter are represented in a letter, the letter must have been written on that typewriter and *only* on that typewriter. No two typewriters can possibly have exactly the same idiosyncrasies.'

'But how does that help us?' asked the superintendent.

'I take it,' said Julian, 'that he didn't produce the letter written to himself until the second interview.'

'That's right.'

'If he'd sent it before, why didn't he produce it when you told him about the others?'

'He may have been frightened to.'

'But he did produce it at the second interview. Why? Are you suggesting that he was so Machiavellian in his plans that he was getting ready to take this very point in his favour in case he were prosecuted?'

'A bit doubtful, I agree.'

'It's not even doubtful. If that was his object, why didn't he instruct counsel to take the point? This letter to himself, dated the 19th September and produced after he knew enquiries were being made, seems to me to make it impossible to believe that he sent any of the letters. You've told me he's an intelligent man. So here we have an intelligent man sending out libellous letters and not wanting to be discovered. Why ask for trouble by writing a letter to himself on his own typewriter after he knew that enquiries were being made, and why does he retain his own typewriter? At the least he could have hidden it until the thing had blown over, or dropped it in the river somewhere, but he let the inspector see it and try it without the slightest hesitation and, if I remember rightly, before this was done he said that he supposed that the inspector wanted to check to see whether the letters had been written on it, and that that could be proved very easily, but he assured him that they weren't.'

'Yes, he said something of the sort.'

'So he knew perfectly well that, if he was the man who wrote the letters, it could be proved against him quite easily. Yet not only did he keep the typewriter but after he knew that enquiries were being made he writes another letter to himself. I say that's quite impossible. If the man was mad and wanted to sacrifice himself because of some feeling of guilt about some conduct of his in the past or that sort of thing, the matter might be different. But you've assured me that he's an absolutely normal man, and I must say that everything he's said to you in the interviews and all his evidence completely confirms your view about him.'

'But who else could have done it?' said the Commissioner.

'That's what we've got to find out,' said Julian. 'And now that the case is over it may be a little easier to make enquiries in the neighbourhood. The real culprit will have a feeling of security. I hope it will be a false one.'

'Why are you so certain about it?' asked the Commissioner.

'Because no other explanation fits with the truth. The vicar's guilt is not consistent with truth. I will go and see him first, if you'll allow me and if he's agreeable. I ought to see for myself that he is the sort of man you say he is. Don't think I'm doubting you in the least. I'm not, but before we go further into the matter I oughtn't to accept anything at second hand that can be proved at first hand.'

The Commissioner didn't reply.

'D'you know, Commissioner,' said Julian, 'I believe you're rather disappointed at what I've said. You've had this thing on your conscience and I believe you'd like me to say that there was no need for it at all and that the vicar was plainly guilty.'

'If I did,' said the Commissioner, 'that's entirely unconscious. I admit that I'm surprised at your conclusions and I shall be very pleased if they turn out to be right.'

'If you can tell me,' said Julian, 'why a man who knows that his crime is being investigated should try to ensure that he will be convicted of it, when that's the last thing in the world that he wants, I might revise my views. It just doesn't make sense. And when what appears to be the truth does not make sense, it is not the truth and we have to look elsewhere for it. Will you arrange for the Home Office to let me and my assistant see him in prison?'

'Of course,' said the Commissioner.

A week later Julian and PM interviewed the vicar.

'I apologise for troubling you,' said Julian, 'but the Commissioner of Police is very worried about your case.'

'I don't understand,' said the vicar. 'He caused me to be prosecuted.'

'He had no alternative. Nevertheless he's extremely worried at the result.'

'Not as much as I am,' said the vicar. 'Or my poor wife. It means ruin for us.'

'That's why we're here,' said Julian. 'The Commissioner wants me to see if there's anything I can do to show that in fact you've suffered an injustice.'

'I have, but I don't see that there's anything more that I can say to you to show it. No one believes me.'

'I hope I'm not giving away confidences,' said Julian, 'but in point of fact the Commissioner and the superintendent both believe you.'

'Then it's quite intolerable that they should have prosecuted me,' said the vicar. 'Is that English fair play? Is that what public men are for? I thought the Public Prosecutor only moved when he was satisfied that a man was guilty. Now you tell me that the Commissioner is satisfied that I wasn't guilty. It seems pretty odd behaviour to me.'

'It must,' said Julian, 'but I will try to explain it to you. I'm sure you must agree that it was the duty of the authorities to try to find out who was responsible for these letters and to prefer a charge against them if they could be found.'

'Of course.'

'Well, everything pointed to the fact that you yourself had written them. Your innocence depended simply upon your word.'

'But you tell me they believed me.'

'How could they be sure that they were right?' said Julian. 'The devil himself knoweth not the thought of man. When I was a judge I believed witnesses I shouldn't have believed and I disbelieved witnesses whom I should have believed.'

'I won't comment on that,' said the vicar. 'At least you have retired.'

PM felt he must stand up for his judge. 'I've never known you wrong, your Honour. Certainly when you believed me you were absolutely right.'

'Every judge is wrong in his beliefs from time to time,' said Julian. 'You have parishioners coming to you for advice. Sometimes you believe their stories and sometimes you don't.'

'I haven't set myself up to judge them or impose penalties on them or ruin them. I am naturally deeply distressed about this whole affair, but when you come to me and say that the people who prosecuted me, the people who sought to prove me guilty of a crime which I wouldn't in any circumstances have committed and which is wholly alien to my nature, that those people now calmly say that they believe I was innocent, I can't think of an adequate comment which would not be unchristian. I'm sorry if it's giving them some bad moments now, but at least they deserve it. I do not.'

'I completely understand your attitude,' said Julian, 'but I take it that, if possible, you would like to be cleared.'

'Of course I would. But how can that be done now? The only way of clearing me was for the Commissioner of Police to say outright and have it published in the newspapers that he was personally satisfied that I'd got nothing to do with it. That is the truth, isn't it?'

'Not entirely,' said Julian. 'The Commissioner only became satisfied after he heard your evidence on oath in the witness box. He personally believes that you were telling the truth. Before that, you had made statements to the superintendent which the Commissioner had only read and, though they read like the truth, he couldn't feel sure about the matter until he'd seen you himself. That in fact is why I'm here now. From what I've read I am convinced in my own mind, if you don't mind my putting it that way, that an intelligent man like yourself who was guilty of this crime could not possibly have behaved in the way in which you did.'

'Perhaps that could be quoted on my tombstone,' said the vicar. 'This really is the last straw. At any rate I hope my wife and I will be able to have a grim laugh about it. What can I do for you, judge, seeing that you've given up

114

believing or disbelieving witnesses and, if you'll allow me to say so, giving wrong judgments from time to time? Are you getting a bit bored and wanting to try your hand on me?'

Julian thought for a moment. 'It isn't quite that, but it's perfectly true that I have got a bit bored since I retired and it's also true that, if I see what appears to have been an injustice, I take great pleasure in righting it. That's the only reason I'm here now. If you'd rather I did nothing more about it and left you at once, of course I'll comply with your wishes.'

'And this gentleman whom you call PM, he is a detective, I think you said?'

'That's right.'

'Employed by the police?'

'No. Privately. He is one of the best men at ascertaining the truth that I've ever met.'

'It's a pity that he didn't come on the scene before,' said the vicar.

'I agree, but that wasn't his fault, nor mine. Now, would you mind if I asked you some questions?'

'I suppose not,' said the vicar.

'How long have you had the typewriter?'

'I've no idea. Some years. Ten or twelve years. It's quite an old one and I bought it second-hand for about £12, I think.'

'Have you ever sent it away to be repaired?'

'Never.'

'Have you ever lent it to anyone?'

'D'you mean to take away?'

'Yes.'

'No, I haven't.'

'But you have let somebody type on it in your house?'

'Only once or twice.'

'Can you remember who those people were? It's important.'

'It's some time ago.'

'When was the last time?'

'I'll have to think. I don't make a note of such things, you'll understand.' He thought for about half a minute. 'Oh yes, I think about a year ago Mrs Pewter said her typewriter had had to go away to be mended and she wanted to type a few letters, so I let her do so.'

'Mrs Pewter?' said Julian. 'Who's she?'

'She runs the shop and post office.'

'A nice woman?'

'She's a very good woman,' said the vicar, 'and if you're going to suggest that she might have typed these letters, the idea is absolutely unthinkable.'

'You say she's a good woman,' said Julian. 'What d'you mean by that?'

'What I say,' said the vicar. 'She's a very useful member of the community and she comes to church regularly.'

'But if you'll forgive my saying so, vicar, I don't think you actually like her very much.'

'That's entirely a personal matter.'

'Do you mean that you've had trouble with her?'

'Trouble? Certainly not. Nothing of the kind. I simply meant that whom I like and dislike and why I like or dislike people is entirely a personal matter for me and I don't propose to discuss it.'

'You don't think you're in her bad books in any way?'

'I'm sure I'm not. I buy most of my groceries there, instead of paying less in the supermarket. I always find her very obliging and she's extremely good at arranging flowers.'

'She's what you would call a good Christian?'

'She is indeed.'

'And so are you, vicar, I take it?'

'What has that got to do with it?'

'Well, you're one good Christian who's been convicted of writing libellous letters. If it wasn't in fact you, why shouldn't it be another good Christian?'

'Too much of a coincidence,' said the vicar. 'Besides, I would count Mrs Pewter as a friend. An enemy has done this.'

'Not necessarily,' said Julian. 'The person who did it is undoubtedly unhinged, but may have no grudge against you. He or she had no particular reason to think that you would be charged with the crime. They couldn't tell if you'd be asked about it even. Somehow or other they had the opportunity of using your typewriter. They may have used it without the slightest wish that you should be suspected of writing the letters but as a safeguard against their being suspected themselves. But tell me something else, vicar, you say that Mrs Pewter arranges the flowers. She does it well, I suppose?'

'Extremely well.'

'Does she like to do it herself or does she get any help?'

'She does it herself.'

'I suppose she's been away sometimes or ill and somebody else has had to do them?'

'Occasionally.'

'Has she ever commented to you on the way they've been done?'

'Women always do that,' said the vicar. 'They all think they can do it better than anyone else.'

'So Mrs Pewter has conveyed to you that she didn't think much of the way the flowers had been done in her absence or something of that kind?'

'I expect so,' said the vicar. 'Possibly that's one reason why I don't take to her very much. It's not a Christian thing to say.'

'How many people do you usually get at morning service?'

'It varies with the time and the weather, but anything from a dozen to thirty. Not so many at early service. Eight or ten's quite good for that.'

'Mrs Pewter comes to both, I imagine.'

'Why d'you say that?' asked the vicar.

'Because you say she's a good Christian.'

'Yes, as a matter of fact she does.'

'D'you remember who else it was who you lent your typewriter to? Or rather who came and used your typewriter?'

'It was a friend of the Bacons, I believe. He was a writer and staying with them and he spent a couple of hours at the vicarage.'

'How long ago was that?'

'Oh, I should say a year or eighteen months. Not less.'

'Have you seen him again since?'

'Yes, he's been down staying with them again.'

'Does he come to church?'

'Only with the Bacons.'

'And how often do they come?'

'Oh, they're quite good. Not every week, but at least once or twice a month.'

'D'you remember what this man's name was?'

'Yes, I do. It was Prendergast. They called him Bill. That's right. Bill Prendergast.'

'Did you see much of him?'

'No, not a lot. I don't see a great deal of the Bacons. They go away a fair amount of the time.'

'They don't lend him their house while they're away?'

'Not as far as I know.'

'Would there be any difficulty in anyone getting into your house while you were out?'

'I can't think why anyone should want to. There's nothing to steal there.'

'So you've never been burgled?'

'Not to my knowledge.'

'D'you leave the doors open when you go out?'

'Usually.'

'So there would be nothing to stop anyone walking in if they wanted to.'

'Apart from burglars – only good manners.'

'You wouldn't mind a friend of yours walking in and waiting for you.'

'Not in the least.'

'Now, please forgive my asking the next question, but it's necessary for me to do so. I haven't yet asked you if you typed the letters. Did you?'

'I did not.'

'When the inspector first came and asked you about them, was it a surprise?'

'A very great surprise. I had no idea there was anybody in the neighbourhood capable of doing a thing like that.'

'When he showed you one or two of the letters, as I think he did, did it ever occur to you that they might have been typed on your typewriter?'

'No, I never thought about it. I mean, to all intents and purposes the type of one typewriter is very like another. I know, of course, that each one is different when you examine the typing carefully, but just to look at a letter merely showed that the typewriter which typed it had a similar typeface.'

'Quite so,' said Julian. 'I think you mentioned that to the inspector when he asked if he could see your typewriter?'

'I don't remember exactly what I said,' said the vicar, 'but I daresay I said something of the sort. I've always known it, I suppose, because it was particularly impressed on my mind by the case of Alger Hiss, who was partly convicted because of a typewriter.'

'What were your feelings when the inspector asked if he could compare the typing in the letters with a specimen from your typewriter?'

'I had no particular feelings at all. I knew that he'd find they didn't tally.'

'And when you found that they did?'

'I must say I was astounded, but I felt at first that it was a coincidence and that closer examination would show that it was a mistake.'

'But when he'd had the results reported on by experts, what did you think then?'

'I didn't know what to think. I don't walk in my sleep and I don't believe that anyone could type a letter in his sleep. I certainly didn't. I hadn't typed the letters, my wife hadn't typed the letters. Who else could have done it?'

'I suppose you were asked whether you ever lent the typewriter and all that sort of thing, as I've asked you today.'

'No doubt, but I don't actually remember all the questions I was asked.'

'Did you mention that Mr Prendergast and Mrs Pewter had come in and used your typewriter?'

'I think I must have, because, knowing that I hadn't done it myself, I had to try and think who else it might have been. But it couldn't have been one of them either. I'd have been bound to have found one of them if they'd come in so often. There were fifteen letters. No, sixteen.'

'They could all have been done at the same time,' said Julian. 'They weren't very long letters. A quick typist could do them in what? About an hour, would you say?'

'Possibly.'

'I'm not for a moment saying that Mrs Pewter typed them,' said Julian, 'but why do you say that she can't have walked in one day and spent an hour typing on your typewriter? If you'd come in, she could have apologised profusely but said that it was very important and, as you'd lent her the typewriter one day, she felt you wouldn't mind. She could only have been convicted of bad manners.'

'Well, I'm sure she didn't.'

'Quite so,' said Julian, 'and I expect you're right. But it is physically possible that she could have.'

'Yes, I suppose it is.'

'And if she could have, somebody else could have.'

'They wouldn't have had the excuse about my letting them use the typewriter.'

'No, but they could have made up some other excuse. I mean this sort of thing. "I do apologise, vicar. I came to see you about something or other." Easy enough to invent something. "I waited a quarter of an hour and then remembered that I had to write a letter to somebody. My handwriting's terribly bad and I thought you mightn't mind my using your typewriter. I do apologise. I assure you I haven't damaged it." Well, you might have been surprised and a bit annoyed, but nothing more than that. And a person who's going to write anonymous libellous letters is going to think out some sort of a story if he or she goes into someone else's house for the purpose of typing them.'

'You really believe that I didn't type the letters?' asked the vicar.

'Yes,' said Julian, 'I do.'

'May I ask why?'

'One of the reasons, curiously enough, is that you're so infernally unpleasant about my trying to help you. A guilty man would have grasped the opportunity with both hands, but you've had enough of the law. You've probably had a great trust in it and it's let you down and, when a retired judge, who didn't always try his cases correctly, barges in on you and starts asking you questions and tells you that the prosecution believed in your innocence, that was really a bit too much.'

'You must have been a better judge than I thought,' said the vicar, 'if I may say so. I apologise for being so surly, but quite frankly we're at our wits' end as to what to do and, when you calmly came and said that I oughtn't to have been prosecuted, it seemed to me to be a bit the limit. I'm sorry. I know you've only come to help.'

'We'll do the best we can,' said Julian, 'won't we, PM?'

'We'll do better than that, sir,' said PM.

'Have you a plan of campaign already?'

'Several,' said PM, 'but it's quite plain what plan we should start on.'

'And that is?'

'The elimination plan,' said PM. 'In a small district like this it's almost bound to work. It's amazing the way it works sometimes in London. The police, to all intents and purposes, know that a crime must have been committed by one of a dozen men, so they proceed to eliminate eleven of them and prosecute the twelfth. That's in a big city of twelve million people. We've only got a couple of thousand to work on and, if you ask me, there'll only be about forty or fifty when we get down to it. You're going to be one short in your congregation, vicar, when we've finished, if I'm not very much mistaken,' he added.

'At the moment it's me,' said the vicar.

'You're eliminated for a start,' said PM. 'Now the next thing is to eliminate Mrs Pewter. I rather like the sound of her. I wish the vicar would say why he didn't like her.'

'All right,' said the vicar, 'I will.'

'Before you do,' said PM, 'might I make a suggestion? She's a bit too domineering and likes her own way? She doesn't like to be criticised?'

'You can say that,' said the vicar.

'She makes a good suspect,' said PM. 'The letters are written by someone like that.'

'I'm quite certain she'd never do such a thing, but perhaps it would be as well not to eliminate her if you think she shouldn't be.'

'You don't understand, vicar,' said Julian. 'When PM says "eliminate" he doesn't mean disregard. On the contrary, he means examine as closely as possible so that, *if* she proves to be in the clear, she's eliminated. That's what elimination means. They only eliminate a criminal without enquiry if he's actually in prison at the time the crime is committed. I take it that Mrs Pewter has never been in prison?'

'Not since I've been in Pendlebury anyway,' said the vicar. 'But she was a prison visitor as a matter of fact, at one time.'

'If you ask me,' said PM, 'Mrs Pewter's going to take a lot of elimination. Churchgoer, dictatorial, vain, likes her own way, and a prison visitor. It's all in the letters, isn't it, your Honour?'

'Nevertheless,' said Julian, 'the vicar's instinct is probably right.'

After a little further conversation the vicar was taken back to his cell and Julian and PM left the prison.

'I leave it to you for the moment, PM,' said Julian, 'but please report to me as soon as you have any news.'

'Of course,' said PM, 'but I shall want a list of names and addresses of all the people who attend church.'

'No doubt the vicar's wife will be able to let us have those,' said Julian.

'Then will you ask her not to leave anyone out,' said PM. 'Even people who only come at Christmas and Easter. Even including them there should be only about fifty or sixty in a place like this.'

PM went home and that night he discussed the matter with AM, that is to say he talked to himself in her presence and occasionally listened to some of her interpolations.

'What would you do?' he asked AM, not intending her to answer.

'Fancy asking me,' said AM. 'All I'm good for is making an omelette.'

'You make a very good omelette,' said PM, 'but I don't see how I can bring that in.'

'It must be awful to be innocent and sent to prison,' said AM. 'I've just been reading about Adolf Beck.'

'What did you say?' said PM.

'I've been reading about Adolf Beck.'

'You've got something there,' said PM. 'My God, you have.'

'What's Adolf Beck got to do with your case? He was convicted of getting money from prostitutes.'

'Quite so. D'you know how his innocence was proved?'

'Yes, of course I do. I've just been reading about it. When they investigated the matter after his second conviction they found that some of the crimes had been committed while he was still in prison.'

'Exactly,' said PM. 'Where's my typewriter?'

'What are you going to do?'   .

'I can't think why I didn't think of it before.' Then he shook his head rather sadly. 'But I'll have to tell the judge and he won't wear it.'

'Won't wear what?'

'If I sent a similar lot of letters out now typed on our typewriter it would appear to show that the person responsible is still at large. It couldn't be the vicar – he's in prison – and it couldn't be typed on his typewriter because that's still held by the court, so the person would have to get hold of another typewriter. They will never discover in a million years that it's mine, and with that additional evidence they ought to get the old boy off.'

'What's wrong with it?' asked AM.

'I tell you, the judge wouldn't allow it. I'd have to tell him and he'd feel personally responsible. He'd say it was concocting evidence.'

'And what would it be?' asked AM.

'Concocting evidence,' said PM. 'But let me think. One of these fifty people in the neighbourhood has done this. One of them has walked into the vicarage while the vicar was out, typed sixteen letters and then sent them out as and when he or she felt inclined. Now, supposing I sent out letters to every one of them? What's going to happen? They should all bring them to the police at once. In the ordinary way some people might hesitate to do so, but, now that the whole thing is public knowledge and the vicar is in prison, they are pretty well bound to bring them to the police and they'll do it quickly because they'll think it proves the vicar's innocence and, because he's a popular figure, they'll be very pleased. Let me think … Tell me, AM, supposing you were the culprit?'

'Me? I wouldn't dream of doing such a thing.'

'I know you wouldn't. But supposing you had? Supposing you'd walked into the vicarage one day when everyone was out and typed out those sixteen letters and sent them off, then you'd have sat back and watched what happened. Eventually you'd have seen the vicar prosecuted and sent to prison. Then suppose you'd suddenly had one of these new letters. What would you do?'

'I'd ask you, of course,' said AM.

'Yes, but supposing you weren't married. Supposing you were a spinster or a widow or a *femme sole*.'

'What a horrible expression. What does it mean?'

'It's normally used to describe a woman who's been divorced or who's divorced her husband.'

'How do you spell it?'

PM spelt it. 'Now don't start talking to me about fish, because this is serious. What would you do if you received one of these letters yourself?'

'Take it to the police, I suppose.'

'Now would you?' said PM. 'Would you if you were the party responsible for sending out the original sixteen letters? Once you go to the police they're going to ask you questions, aren't they? You've never been asked questions about the other sixteen letters yet. You know you wrote them all. You know that somebody else is in prison for your crime, so you don't want to be asked any questions at all. If you just throw the letter away or say nothing about it you can't be asked any questions. Isn't that what you'd want to do?'

'I wouldn't know what to do.'

'I'm not talking about you,' said PM.

'I thought you were,' said AM.

'We're pretending for the moment that you were the person who wrote the original letters.'

'Oh yes, of course. I really should stick to making omelettes. I'm no use at solving your problems.'

'You've been a great deal of use,' said PM. 'Adolf Beck was an inspiration. Now, if you just keep quiet about the letter, I mean the new letter, nobody will come and ask you anything about it.'

'So I keep very quiet about it,' said AM. 'What then?'

'Then I shall send you another letter and perhaps another and perhaps in the third one – I'll have to think this over – but perhaps in the third one I'll make some threatening remark about the earlier letters. Now what d'you do? If you go to the police now, you know you'll be asked why you didn't bring in the other two. And you don't like the idea of that at all, particularly as you wrote the original letters. So again I think you're going to do nothing. But, if you do nothing after the third letter, it proves conclusively that you must be the person responsible for the earlier letters. I would say so anyway. Then all we have to do is to go and collect the fruit.'

'Collect the fruit?' said AM.

'Stand under the tree,' said PM, 'until it drops into our arms. It may be necessary to shake the tree a little, but that's all, and if this comes off,' said PM, 'it will be thanks to you.'

'And what do I get?' said AM.

'You can have this on account,' said PM and kissed her.

Before typing and sending off the letters PM got Julian's approval to the scheme. Within a week fifty-one people in the neighbourhood had received a letter which was similar in terms to those which had been the subject-matter of the charge against the vicar. Most of the recipients brought the letters to the police station within a few days. One or two of them were away, but brought them on their return. When the first letters were brought in, the superintendent telephoned Julian.

'Something very exciting has happened,' he said. 'The letters have started all over again on a different typewriter. That shows it can't have been the vicar.'

'I'm sorry to disappoint you,' said Julian, and explained what had happened. 'What is important is to know how many people have brought in the letters.'

'There are thirty so far,' said the superintendent.

'Please let me know how it goes on,' said Julian. 'Fifty-one letters have been sent out and what we're hoping is that only fifty letters will be brought in.'

Three weeks later the superintendent telephoned Julian. 'I think we've had the lot,' he said.

'Fifty-one?' said Julian.

'I think so, but I'll just count them again.' He started counting to himself – 'forty-seven, forty-eight, forty-nine, fifty ... By Jove,' he said, 'there's one missing.'

'Better count them again,' said Julian, 'to be on the safe side.' The superintendent did so.

'No,' he said, 'I was wrong. We've got the lot.'

Julian thought for a moment. Then he asked, 'How many of them sent them or brought them more than a week after they'd received them without the excuse of having been on holiday?'

'If you'd hold on, I can tell you that,' said the superintendent.

'Could I have their names, please?'

'Of course.'

'And if they sent them in, the terms of any covering letter.'

'Hold on.'

A few minutes later the superintendent was able to tell Julian that there were four people who were late in sending in the letters. Their names were Mr Tweedie, Mrs Wallet, Miss Knibb and Mrs Pewter. 'Miss Knibb sent a letter,' said the superintendent, 'in the following terms: Here is a letter which I have just received. I suppose the parson's wife could type after all and is carrying on the good work, but, unless she goes on with it, I personally don't want her prosecuted. I think that she and her husband have suffered enough and that a warning to her would be sufficient.'

'How late was she in sending the letter?'

'A fortnight.'

'I'm very much obliged,' said Julian. 'I'll ask Mrs Kingsdown about the four of them.'

Julian already knew about Mrs Wallet and Mrs Pewter. He was told by Mrs Kingsdown that Mr Tweedie was a difficult man, but unlikely to have written to anyone anonymously and that Miss Knibb was a perfectly ordinary spinster with no particular 'isms' of which Mrs Kingsdown was aware.

'Has she been away in the last month?' asked Julian.

'No,' said Mrs Kingsdown, 'she hasn't.'

'Thank you,' said Julian, and made a mental note to consider why Miss Knibb should have said that she had *just* received the letter when in fact she had had it for fourteen days.

He decided that he would enlist the help of the parson who had been sent to hold the fort until a new incumbent could be found for the Pendlebury living, and he and PM called at the vicarage where the Reverend Angus Perryman was temporarily installed.

CHAPTER SEVEN

Another Parson

The Reverend Angus Perryman was being groomed for
stardom. At the time when the vicar of Pendlebury was
sent to prison the living which Perryman's bishop had in
mind for him was not vacant, though it was likely to be
in the near future. Accordingly the bishop asked him
whether he would act as a stop-gap at Pendlebury and he
readily agreed. He had most of the qualities desirable in a
parson. He was intelligent, kind and, if a conceited person
can be humble, he was that too. He was not in the least
vain, that is to say he did not worry about what sort of a
figure he cut or what other people thought of him. He was
infinitely humble before his God, but he was sufficiently
intelligent to know roughly where he stood among men.
If pressed by a close friend to describe himself as a
preacher he would have said, 'good second-rate'. This in
fact was very high praise indeed, for the number of first-
rate preachers is very small. First-rate is often a much
abused word. It is a very high standard indeed to say of a
man, for example, that he is a first-rate lawyer and it *should*
mean that he is of the calibre of Lord Atkin or Lord
Tomlin. There are not many of them around. So a good
second-rate parson could easily aspire to a bishopric, and
it was not only Perryman's bishop who had this in mind

for him. He had another distinction which was of his own making. He was well-to-do. He had always wanted to be ordained, but knowing that the financial position of many parsons was little short of a disgrace to the congregation for whom they provided comfort and understanding, he had decided that he could not satisfactorily undertake the duties of a parson if half the time he and his wife were having to consider how to find the money to clothe their children or to keep themselves in reasonable comfort.

He therefore had to make sufficient money to support himself and a wife and any children in satisfactory conditions for, say, the next twenty or thirty years. He had left school without any particular qualifications except that of a good second-rate intelligence. So he decided to write a bestseller. With this in view, he read many of the current bestsellers. He found that most of them dealt in sexual activities of one kind or another and violence. As he had no intention whatever of writing about these subjects himself, he analysed the reasons why the authors of these books had relied so much upon these subjects. He came to the conclusion without much difficulty that most readers identify themselves with one or more of the characters in the book which they are reading. He also knew that most human beings had at least a touch of sadism or masochism in them. They were thus able to get enormous pleasure by identifying themselves with James Bond and enjoying the risks involved in his amatory and other adventures without any danger of being shot by the secret police of a foreign nation or being found by their wives in compromising circumstances. Mr Perryman decided that he must write a book in which the characters could be found in any ordinary home. To write a successful book an author must have a discerning eye or a discerning ear, so that he can fill it with dialogue or descriptions which will interest and amuse the reader. Perryman had both the eye and the ear. There is nothing humdrum in life if you have the ear to pick up the humour of it or the eye to see the absurdities. Accordingly, all the people in Mr Perryman's book were going to see themselves as interesting and amusing men and women. Most writers can describe a scene of sexual enjoyment with or without variations or a vicious fight. If they do it well, their books will sell in thousands or millions, but the readers know that, although they may imagine themselves doing all the things which James Bond did, they will never in fact do them. In the book which Perryman intended to write, readers could do all the things which the characters in his book did. Identification could be complete.

So he wrote his book and he called it *Mum Says*. It was an immediate success on both sides of the Atlantic and it was soon made into a television series which Mr Perryman hoped, though without much confidence, would still be running when he became a bishop. As soon as his financial position was secure he went into a theological college and in due course was ordained. At the time he was asked to act as a stop-gap at Pendlebury he was aged forty, married to a charming and sensible wife called Joan and had two children, a boy and a girl, aged eight and ten.

Julian and PM called on Mr Perryman just after he had finished preparing his sermon for the next Sunday. Julian explained the reason for their visit.

'I have no doubt,' he said, 'that an injustice has been done, but we shall never be able to put that right unless we can find the real person who sent the letters. He or she must be a member of your congregation and all I am asking you to do at the moment is to invite the whole of your congregation next Sunday to come and have a drink with you at the vicarage. This will enable me and my assistant to talk to some of the people and with luck to eliminate those whom I do not think can have been involved.'

'I am not sure that I like the idea of luring my parishioners into a trap,' said Perryman.

'It's hardly that,' said Julian. 'If none of them is guilty, he or she has nothing to fear. On the other hand, if the guilty party is among them, surely it's in the interests of the Church and the public that the innocent man in prison should be released as soon as possible. I understand your objection to inviting your congregation to come and be looked over by me, as it were, with a view to discovering whether any one of them is a criminal, but I should have thought you would have had a far greater objection to the gross injustice which has been perpetrated. If my view about that is right, there is a member of your congregation who is well aware that a good man has been unjustly imprisoned and who is doing nothing whatever about it. Isn't it right that he or she should be encouraged to do something about it? And I suggest that a party and a couple of glasses of sherry are a very mild form of persuasion.'

'All right,' said Mr Perryman, after he'd thought about the matter for a minute or two. 'I'll give the party but I will take no part in any conversation designed to produce evidence against the offender.'

'Why not?' said Julian. 'Surely you'd help to catch a burglar. This person has done far more harm than stealing something from a dwelling-house. I don't want you to take part in any specific conversation, only to introduce me and PM to the other people at the party. We will do the rest.'

Mr Perryman eventually agreed and on the following Sunday, when he'd completed his sermon, he said this:

'Although it is true that I am only likely to be here for some months, I should very much like to get to know you and to give you the opportunity of getting to know me as well as possible during that period. I should therefore be delighted if you would all come to the vicarage after the service and have a glass of sherry with me.'

After the service was over Mr Perryman stood in the door of the church and greeted the congregation as they filed out.

'I hope you will be coming across to the vicarage,' he said to each of them, and nearly all of them said that they would be delighted to do so. But Mrs Wallet said that she was afraid she could not come.

'My husband is waiting for me at home,' she explained.

'I'm sorry he could not be here this morning,' said Mr Perryman.

'Not be here?' said Mrs Wallet. 'Of course he was here.'

'I'm so sorry,' said Mr Perryman. 'He must have slipped out while I was in the vestry. But I'm sorry he couldn't stay. I hope you will both come another time.'

'Wine is a mocker,' said Mrs Wallet.

'Ah,' said Mr Perryman, 'but what about your stomach's sake?'

'That's quite unnecessary in this country. St Paul was speaking about a country where the water was more subject to pollution than it is here today.'

'Well, I hope a couple of glasses of sherry are not going to do anyone any harm this morning,' said Mr Perryman.

'They aren't going to do me any harm,' said Mrs Wallet. 'Good morning.' And she walked off.

There had been twenty people at morning service and Julian had to admit to himself that he was less concerned with his devotions on that occasion than with trying to form some impression of them from their appearances, though he knew from experience that an impression of appearance is often a very bad guide. Both as a barrister and as a judge he had often been mistaken in his judgment of a person by his or her appearance only. He remembered particularly one occasion when a thorough-paced villain had been mentioned by counsel in his opening of a case and when he had looked round the court to try to find him. He eventually, as he thought, identified him as the man sitting next to the solicitor instructing counsel. An evil-looking man, he thought. He probably drinks too much and is the sort of man who would run over his old mother. It turned out in the end that the man cast by him as the villain of the piece was the highly respectable and kindly solicitor in the case and that the real villain was the man next to him, who looked the sort of man who, when driving a car, would always give way to a pedestrian who wanted to cross the road.

Before the party Julian and PM had discussed the matter.

'The person who wrote those letters,' said Julian, 'was known to the vicar sufficiently well to be able to call on him, was, I would say, a regular churchgoer, quite well educated and had been in the neighbourhood some little time, and probably lived alone. I gather that Mrs Pewter, Mrs Wallet, Miss Knibb and Mr Tweedie all have the necessary qualifications so, unless we find someone else equally interesting, we'd better investigate them first.'

The party was soon going well. Joan Perryman and her two children had seen to that. There are three attributes of a successful party, enough drink, enough food and enough noise. A party at which you can hear what is being said to you is a failure from the start. Julian remembered going to a highly successful party where it was practically impossible to hear anything that was said to him. It was at the house of an ex-Army friend who had become a writer. The host introduced a man to Julian and left them. Julian started the conversation by asking the man as loudly as he could if he were a writer. Julian could lip-read that he said 'No'. 'You were in the Army perhaps?' said Julian. Once again he could lip-read that the answer was 'Good God, no.' And then the man added, as Julian thought: 'I'm a Jew, but there's not much in it these days.' While Julian was wondering whether to reply that he was sorry to hear that or that none of his Jewish friends had mentioned it to him, he suddenly realised that he must have misheard what was said. 'Where is your dukedom?' he shouted and he was right. It was the Duke of Dorset.

As soon as he was able to, Julian tackled Mr Tweedie. 'How long have you been here, Mr Tweedie?' he asked.

'Too long.'

This answer was sufficient to encourage Julian to invite Mr Tweedie to come into the garden and have a chat where they could hear each other better. Mr Tweedie readily agreed.

'I hate these parties,' he said.

'I thought it rather a nice idea,' said Julian.

'At any rate the sherry's better than I expected,' said Mr Tweedie. 'But the people – ' and he waved his hand in a way which was intended to indicate disgust.

'I don't really know them,' said Julian.

'Some people have all the luck.'

'Might I ask why you don't leave the neighbourhood then?'

'Probably be worse anywhere else. Wherever you go, you're bound to find members of the human race.'

'Would you prefer to live in a zoo?' asked Julian.

'I wouldn't mind,' said Mr Tweedie, 'but you'd have to mix with the keepers, I suppose.'

'Why don't you like people?'

'Because they bore me,' said Mr Tweedie. 'Look at all the words that are being spoken inside there at the moment. How many of them are worth saying?'

'They can't be heard anyway,' said Julian. 'I wonder if I might ask you rather an impertinent question?' And without waiting for permission he went on, 'I gather you're a regular churchgoer here.'

'It's the only place where I can get a bit of quiet,' said Mr Tweedie, 'and I'll say one thing for the late parson. He preached a damned good sermon.'

'I wonder what made him write those letters,' said Julian.

'I don't believe he did,' said Mr Tweedie.

'Who else could have done it?'

'If I knew, I wouldn't say,' said Mr Tweedie. 'Or they could have me for slander. They could, couldn't they?'

'Not if you could prove it,' said Julian.

'Yes, but how on earth can you do that?'

'But how could anyone else have written the letters on the vicar's typewriter?'

'Simple enough,' said Mr Tweedie. 'Just walk into the vicarage and type them out.'

'You think someone did that?'

'I'm sure of it.'

'Any idea who?'

'Certainly, but I'm not saying.'

'It wasn't you, I suppose?'

'No,' said Mr Tweedie, 'but it could have been if I'd been minded that way. I'm not, as a matter of fact. My particular idiosyncrasy is to be rude to people's faces. I like to watch the reaction. If I may say so, you seem to be a little like that too. Asking a perfect stranger if he'd written those letters. That's more the sort of thing that I'd be likely to say.'

'I do apologise,' said Julian.

'Ah, there's the difference,' said Mr Tweedie. 'I wouldn't have.'

Julian next persuaded Mrs Pewter to come into the garden with him and soon turned to the subject of the letters. Mrs Pewter also doubted whether the vicar could have written them.

'He was not that sort of man,' she said.

'Who else could have done it?'

'If you ask me,' said Mrs Pewter, 'there's only one person who could have done it and she's not here.'

'You mean – ?' said Julian.

'She's as mad as a hatter,' said Mrs Pewter.

'But why hasn't something been done about it?' said Julian. 'It's awful to think of the vicar being in prison and going to be unfrocked for something he didn't do.'

'We all think that,' said Mrs Pewter, 'but what can we do about it?'

'The only way to find out,' said Julian, 'is to ask everybody who might have done it whether he or she did do it.'

'But you're not going to get the truth out of them. Who on earth would admit it? If I'd done it, I assure you I wouldn't.'

'Could you visualise yourself as doing such a thing?' asked Julian.

'Certainly not,' said Mrs Pewter.

The party was still in full swing when Julian suggested to PM that he should make an excuse for leaving and go and see Mrs Wallet. 'Meanwhile,' he said, 'I'll occupy myself with Miss Knibb.'

Miss Knibb was a spinster of fifty-five and the information which Julian had been given that she was quite normal was confirmed by her conversation. But the 'just received' in her letter made him anxious to probe into her more deeply. A person with a guilty conscience might hesitate about sending in the letter, as it might result in her being questioned by the police. And then, having decided it was better to send it in, such a person might try to avoid the appearance of delay by putting 'just'. It was a small point but worth investigating.

So he made himself sufficiently agreeable to Miss Knibb to obtain an invitation to tea with her. While he was engaged in doing this PM had reached Mrs Wallet's house.

CHAPTER EIGHT

Mrs Wallet ·

He stumped his way up to the front door and rang the bell.

'Mrs Wallet?' he said, when she answered it.

'I'm glad you've come,' she said. 'I hate waiting. You're happily married, I hope?'

'Very,' said PM.

'Good. That will save a lot of trouble. I find that some single men are inclined to worship the ground I walk on.'

'Well, you seem to have about two acres,' said PM. 'And that's pretty valuable these days. D'you happen to have planning permission?'

'A man after my own heart,' said Mrs Wallet, 'but I'm afraid there can be no question of a liaison. I'm married to my God and he doesn't permit that sort of liberty.'

'Nor does my wife,' said PM.

'Ah, but there's a difference,' said Mrs Wallet. 'Your wife wouldn't know. My God would.'

'You have a point there,' said PM. 'Don't you find it awkward sometimes?'

'Never. It makes it so much easier. If every husband knew for certain that his wife would know what he was doing and every wife knew for certain that her husband would know what she was doing, it would make life so much simpler. And he's very considerate,' she added. 'I get two half-days a week and in addition three weeks' holiday in the year.'

'Might I ask what you do with yourself then? Write letters, by any chance?'

'Oh, I do write rather a lot of letters, but I wouldn't do that in the holidays.'

'Might I ask how you do occupy yourself during the three weeks and the half-days?'

'Have fun,' said Mrs Wallet.

'What sort of fun?'

'Things I can't do the rest of the year.'

'Like making mischief?' queried PM.

'Making mischief is certainly very good fun. Yes, I do do a bit of that sometimes.'

'Might I ask why you're telling me all this?' said PM.

'It's quite simple. My husband told me you would be coming,' said Mrs Wallet. 'He also told me that I should find you a kindred spirit and that he would have no objection to our putting our heads together.'

'Might I ask you one thing?' said PM. 'I understood from someone that you were a widow.'

'Widow?' said Mrs Wallet. 'Good gracious no. Didn't I tell you that my husband spoke to me about you?'

'Yes, indeed,' said PM, 'but that, I gather, was the Almighty.

'He doesn't like to be called that,' said Mrs Wallet. 'You see, he's not, as a matter of fact. It would save an awful lot of misunderstanding if people realised that.'

'Are you by any chance referring to Mr Wallet?' asked PM.

'Oh heavens, no. He died a few years back. Six or seven, I should say. Naturally I waited a year or two before marrying again. But of course I'd known my present husband for most of my life, so we weren't exactly strangers to one another.'

'Does your husband know that the vicar of this parish is at present in prison?'

'Indeed, yes,' said Mrs Wallet. 'He said the mortification of the flesh will be good for him. He was having too easy a time here. He has something of the sort in mind for a good number of parsons. There's one bishop my husband particularly is thinking of, two as a matter of fact. He doesn't think nine months would do either of them any harm. But of course he's not all that sure and he doesn't want to make a mistake.'

'Mistake?' said PM. 'Does your husband make mistakes?'

'Oh good gracious, yes, of course,' said Mrs Wallet. 'I told you that Almighty is a complete misnomer. I won't say that he makes mistakes like everyone else, because his mistakes are on a larger scale, but I may tell you in confidence that he didn't intend either of the last two World Wars. He was quite upset about them, particularly the first.'

'You don't happen to have any of his writing paper in the house, do you?'

'I've run out, I'm afraid,' said Mrs Wallet. 'I must order some more.'

'Has he, by any chance, written any books?'

'The Bible, you mean,' said Mrs Wallet. 'He didn't write that. That's full of mistakes. The story of Solomon, for example.'

'The two women and the baby and the sword, d'you mean?'

'Exactly.'

'I thought it was rather good,' said PM. 'What's wrong with it?'

142

'The butter's spread too thick,' said Mrs Wallet. 'When the two women each claimed the baby and Solomon sent for the sword, the real mother said, "Give it to her rather than kill it." That's all right so far and, if the story had stopped there and Solomon had given the child to her, no one would have complained. But it doesn't, you see. The false mother says, "Let it be neither mine nor thine but divide it." How on earth could she have said that if she wanted the baby? When the real mother said, "Give it to her" she would have accepted it gladly and said, "I'm glad she's seen the light" and that would have been that, but to say that she wanted the baby to be cut in half when it had been offered to her whole and when her claim to the baby was the sole reason they were in front of Solomon, is utter nonsense. My husband would never have written a thing like that.'

'D'you think the vicar was guilty of writing all those letters?'

'That may have been one of my husband's mistakes. Someone else might have written them.'

'You didn't, I suppose?'

'Good gracious no! Whatever could have made you think that?'

'Oh, I didn't,' said PM. 'I was being facetious.'

'My husband is never facetious,' said Mrs Wallet. 'That's what I like about him. He's got a fine sense of humour but he's never facetious.'

CHAPTER NINE

Another Candidate

That evening Julian discussed with PM the material which they had collected.

'Mrs Wallet is an obvious possibility,' said Julian, 'because she's a lunatic. On the other hand, from the conversation you had with her the letters don't seem to me to be in her style somehow. They're a little too sanely written, if you follow what I mean. From the way she talked to you, I doubt whether she could write sixteen letters at a go of the type we've read. She couldn't have resisted mentioning her husband in one or other of them. It seems to me that she really is just mad, whereas the writer of the letters is bad as well as mad. My friend Mr Tweedie is a possible candidate because he hates the whole human race, and he likes being offensive to them and watching the effect. On the other hand, he didn't seem to have a power complex. He likes to be rude to people and watch their faces. He'd see nothing by going to church and watching people obeying his orders. He's mad too, of course, but I doubt if he's really bad. But still he is a possibility. We can't rule him out. Now, although Mrs Pewter has all the qualifications for a suspect, if I'm any judge of character at all she's had nothing to do with it. She's really sorry for the vicar.'

'Then why didn't she do anything about it?' said PM.

'People who run the local shop can't do anything about that sort of thing. Their job is to be nice to everyone and not to do anything which is likely to offend any part of the community. They want everybody as a customer, so they can't start petitions or do anything of that sort. I'm certainly satisfied in my own mind that it's not Mrs Pewter.'

'Pity,' said PM. 'I'd been looking forward to proving it against her.'

'That will be a problem,' said Julian. 'Even if I'm satisfied that it is one of them, it will be quite another matter to get the evidence.'

'I'm not so sure. Once you tell me who it is, I think I'll get the evidence for you. But only if you're right. I rely on you for that.'

'In other words,' said Julian, 'you're saying that, if you fail to get the evidence, it will be because I'm wrong in my judgment.'

'I couldn't have put it better,' said PM.

The following afternoon Julian kept his appointment with Miss Knibb at Riverbank House. She opened the door herself and took him straight into the sitting-room.

'What a charming place you have.'

'It is nice, isn't it. I do most of the gardening myself, but old Garrett gives me a hand every now and then.'

'If I may say so,' said Julian, 'you both make a very good job of it.'

'D'you like lemon or milk with your tea?'

'Milk, if I may.'

'Of course. So do I. But, when I have strangers to tea, I always have lemon just in case. Are you staying here long?'

'Only a few days,' said Julian. 'The vicar very kindly invited me.'

'The vicar?' said Miss Knibb. 'I thought he was in jail.'

'I should have said the acting vicar,' said Julian. 'What a charming man he is.'

'I never really knew the last one,' said Miss Knibb. 'I found it very difficult to get to know him properly. I suppose it's natural. They have to keep a sort of protective veneer around them. They get to know us all right, but we rarely get to know them. Haven't you found that?'

'I suppose you're right,' said Julian, 'except in the case of a personal friend. I've one or two parsons who are personal friends and that's rather different.'

'Of course.'

'It must have been very shattering for the parish,' said Julian, 'to have their vicar taken away from them.'

'It was indeed. A shocking thing. I would never have believed it of him.'

'But that's always the case, isn't it?' said Julian. 'When somebody does something rather terrible, nine-tenths of the people who knew him or her say, "I wouldn't have believed it possible." '

'I suppose so,' said Miss Knibb.

'I didn't follow the trial myself,' said Julian. 'It was proved, I suppose?'

'Proved? Oh, good heavens, yes. Up to the hilt. That was the rather sad thing about it because in court he denied it all. On oath too. That was bad for a parson. What one expected was that he'd plead guilty and call medical evidence that he'd been under a terrible strain or something of that sort. That's what's usually done in these sort of cases.'

'Funny you should say that,' said Julian. 'Mrs Pewter thought he wasn't guilty.'

'Mrs Pewter?' said Miss Knibb. 'Well, it's rather natural really. She has to think well of everybody. Not an easy job running a village shop with two supermarkets not five miles away.'

'What was he like?'

'The late vicar, d'you mean?'

'Yes.'

'Oh, quite ordinary. I wonder why he did it. Religious mania of some kind. Probably doing too much and it preyed on his nerves.'

After a short further discussion on the case Julian felt that he was getting nowhere except for the fact that Miss Knibb never mentioned the letter which PM had sent to her. Why not? He turned to other subjects. Miss Knibb read quite a lot, was fond of music and there was no difficulty in holding a perfectly civilised conversation with her. Indeed Julian quite enjoyed it. After about three-quarters of an hour he eventually got up to go.

'It's been most kind of you to have me to tea.'

'Not at all,' said Miss Knibb. 'I've enjoyed it. If you're staying longer, I hope you'll come again.'

'As a matter of fact,' said Julian, 'I might stay a little longer. I've been asked to make enquiries in the neighbourhood.'

'Enquiries?' said Miss Knibb. 'About what?'

'About the letters.'

'But the vicar sent them.'

'I mean in case he didn't.'

'If he didn't,' said Miss Knibb, 'who did?'

'You didn't, I suppose?' said Julian.

'Me? Why on earth should *I* want to send them? What an extraordinary question to ask.'

'But did you?' asked Julian.

'Look,' said Miss Knibb, 'I'm an ordinary, respectable woman who lives in the neighbourhood, I pay my bills and I go to church. I cause trouble to no one. Why on earth should I do a thing like that?'

'Why, indeed? Thank you so very much again for having me to tea,' and Julian left.

PM was waiting for him outside the vicarage. 'I thought you might want to have a chat alone,' he said.

'I do indeed.'

'What was Miss Knibb like?'

'Very pleasant, very ordinary, very normal,' said Julian. 'Now it's up to you to find the evidence against her.'

'What? Are you sure it's her?'

'Yes, I am. I had a feeling about her and I took a chance and it came off.'

'What came off?'

'I asked her if she'd sent the letters and she wouldn't deny it.'

'She wouldn't deny it?' said PM with a lot of surprise in his voice.

'Possibly you haven't had the same experience, PM,' said Julian, 'but every criminal lawyer will tell you this. That, when you ask a guilty man the straight question whether he's stolen something or other, the chances are that he will say, "What should I want to steal it for?" Or use words to that effect. There are two reasons for this. First of all, he funks the straight denial for some curious reason. Secondly, he feels that the straight denial is insufficient. Knowing that he is guilty he feels that he's got to back up his declaration of innocence by something more than a mere "No". The person who's completely innocent will deny the charge at once and then possibly add the reasons for his innocence later. But the guilty person parries the question as long as he can for the two reasons that I have mentioned. Miss Knibb didn't even say "No" when I asked her the second time. Twice she said in effect, "What should I want to steal it for?" '

'But, surely, that couldn't be used as evidence against her in court?'

'Of course not. *You've* got to get the *evidence*.'

CHAPTER TEN

The End of the Chase

Two days later Miss Knibb was surprised to receive a letter typed on PM's typewriter. It read as follows:

> The Seat of Knowledge,
> Pendlebury,
> Kent.

Dear Miss Knibb,

What does it feel like to be safe and secure while someone else is in prison for your crime? Do you think God is still on your side? He must be moving in a very mysterious way if he is, don't you think? How are you sleeping these days? Any bad dreams? And what makes you think that I won't give you away? I'll tell you one way of making sure that I do. That is, if you go to the police. If you do go to them, I shall tell them how I saw you walk into the vicarage one day not long before the first letter was written, ring the bell, wait and knock and eventually when there was no answer walk in. I saw you come out an hour later with the letters in your bag. Oh no, I didn't see them in your bag. But what were you doing in the vicarage all by yourself for an hour? If you want to be sure that *I* go to the police, *you* go to them with this letter.

Yours sincerely,

ILL-WISHER NO.2.

Having discovered that Miss Knibb did not take that letter to the police within a week of receiving it, PM wrote to her again. This letter read as follows:

> The Seat of Knowledge,
> Pendlebury,
> Kent.

Dear Miss Knibb,

I'm so glad you've been sensible. I have a proposition to make to you, and I should like to come and call upon you to make it. If you are prepared to receive me, please insert a small advertisement in the personal column of *The Collinson & District Gazette* to say the time and date when I may call upon you and don't make it too long ahead, please. By all means invite the police to be present if you wish and, if you do, I shall have an interesting story to tell them. If you don't, we should have a pleasant little chat.

Yours sincerely,

ILL-WISHER NO.2.

The next issue of *The Collinson & District Gazette* contained an advertisement inserted by Miss Knibb, 'Tuesday 4 o'clock'. PM attended exactly at that time. Miss Knibb opened the door to him.

'How d'you do?' said PM. 'How nice of you to invite me in. Don't let's bother about introductions. I know your name. You don't know mine and there's no need that you should.' She took him into the sitting-room. He sat down.

'Forgive me sitting before I'm asked,' he said. 'It's as well to start as we mean to go on.'

'So you're the man who's been writing these ridiculous letters,' said Miss Knibb.

'That's me,' said PM.

'And what d'you think to gain by it?'

'That depends on you,' said PM. 'But I don't think there should be any difficulty between us.' Then he waited until Miss Knibb found the silence unendurable.

'What you write,' she said, 'is absolutely untrue and I can prove it.'

'Prove away,' said PM.

'If you did see me go into the vicarage – which I didn't – why didn't you come forward before and tell the police?'

'For the simple reason,' said PM, 'that then I should not have been able to have this very pleasant little conversation with you.'

There was again a silence but this time PM broke it. 'You haven't yet asked me what I am.'

'Well, what are you?'

'I scrape a living,' said PM, 'by finding out other people's secrets and bleeding them white.'

'A blackmailer,' said Miss Knibb.

'Some people don't like the term,' said PM, 'but I don't mind it at all. The late Sir Alan Herbert said that, if there weren't something black, there would be nothing to blackmail anybody about. Rather good, don't you think?'

'I've no money but what I need for my living purposes,' said Miss Knibb.

'But,' said PM, 'you could live in rather more straitened circumstances, could you not? Change to margarine, for instance, and instead of those holidays in Switzerland try Southend or possibly don't go for a holiday at all. But I'm not unreasonable, I won't take much more than you can afford.'

'You won't take anything at all,' said Miss Knibb angrily.

'You're quite right,' said PM, 'I won't *take* anything but, if from the goodness of your heart you choose to give me something, I shall gratefully accept.'

'How much d'you want?' said Miss Knibb.

'I prefer to leave it to the customer,' said PM, 'then you can't complain that I've overcharged you.'

'What would happen if I don't pay you anything?'

'I should simply go to the police and tell them what I saw. And the rest will be up to them.'

'I shall deny it,' said Miss Knibb. 'Why should they believe you and not me?'

'Why, indeed? Word against word. A blackmailer on the one side and a highly respectable member of the community on the other, it looks bad for me, doesn't it.' He paused for a moment and then added: 'You're in rather a strong position really, Miss Knibb. I shouldn't pay me very much, if I were you. What about a pound a week?'

Miss Knibb could hardly keep the relief which she felt at the smallness of the amount out of her voice when she said, 'A pound a week?'

'Or is that too much?'

'I could just manage a pound,' said Miss Knibb.

'Right,' said PM. 'A pound it is. I shall be in the neighbourhood for a week or two, so perhaps I'd better call at the same time each week. Then when I leave I will give you an address to send it to. Will that be all right?'

'Very well,' said Miss Knibb.

'Let's have the first pound then, please. I'll give you a receipt and then, if you get tired of paying, you can always take it to the police to prove I've had it. Perhaps you'd let me have a piece of paper.'

Miss Knibb handed him a piece of paper and on it PM wrote, 'Received from Miss Knibb one pound for my silence. Ill-Wisher No.2.'

'I nearly forgot to add the No.2,' he said. 'I'm so glad this interview has gone off so pleasantly. Sometimes people are much more difficult. I'm so grateful to you for making it so easy. I'll be here again next Thursday at the same time.'

'Well, your Honour,' said PM later that evening to Julian. 'You were right and so am I. If she doesn't report my visit within a week, I suggest the superintendent or some police officer should accompany me to Miss Knibb but he shouldn't come in for ten minutes. I can take another pound off her in that ten minutes and give her a receipt. Then I shall have a little chat, there will be a knock at the door and Bob's your uncle.'

'That seems fair enough,' said Julian.

A week later PM called on Miss Knibb, and the superintendent himself, with an inspector, waited a little way down the road.

'May I come in?' said PM, when Miss Knibb opened the door. 'I'd like to have a little chat. No, don't worry, I don't want to put up the charges.'

Miss Knibb took him into the sitting-room and he sat down.

'I'm very well, thank you. As a matter of fact I'm better than that. You'll be glad to hear that I'm in fine fettle. I put that pound of yours on a horse and it won. It made me ten pounds, thank you very much. Have you ever tried racing yourself?'

'No,' said Miss Knibb.

'Can I have the second pound? If I'm as lucky with that as I was with the first, I shan't be doing badly. I almost offered to share the winnings with you.'

Miss Knibb handed him a pound and a piece of paper for the receipt. PM wrote out a similar receipt to the first and handed it to her. He put the pound in his pocket. For once PM couldn't think of anything to say and he had to while away a few minutes before the police arrived.

'Nice weather for the time of year,' he said.

'Very,' said Miss Knibb.

'I shall be going away in a day or two,' said PM, 'so I'll get you to send the pound each week to an address I'll give you. You'd better send a postal order and don't forget to cross it, then it doesn't matter if it's lost. I don't like sending treasury notes through the post and it's so expensive to register them.'

'Very well,' said Miss Knibb, and she added: 'How long is this going on for?'

'What would you think would be reasonable?' said PM. 'You've behaved very fairly, so I'm quite prepared to reciprocate. Would you think a year too long?'

Again Miss Knibb had difficulty in repressing excitement from her voice.

'A year?' she said. 'That would mean fifty-two pounds.'

'With the two pounds you paid me, fifty pounds.'

'Suppose,' said Miss Knibb, hesitantly, 'suppose – suppose I paid you fifty pounds in a lump sum, would that settle the matter once and for all?'

'What a good idea,' said PM. 'It would save these visits or save your having to send it by post. Yes, I think that's an excellent idea. I think it's very kind of you to have suggested it. When could you let me have it?'

'I'd have to cash a cheque,' said Miss Knibb, 'but I could do it tomorrow.'

'That would be splendid,' said PM and at that moment there was a knock at the door. Miss Knibb answered it.

'I'm Superintendent Carson of the CID,' said the superintendent, 'and this is Inspector Hiscock. Might we come in for a moment?'

Miss Knibb let them in.

'I understand from this gentleman,' said the superintendent, when they were all in the sitting-room, 'that you have agreed to pay a pound a week to him. Would you mind telling me why?'

'I haven't agreed to any such thing,' said Miss Knibb.

PM opened his bag and produced his tape recorder. 'This is a tape recorder, Miss Knibb,' he said, 'in case you don't know it. Shall I play over our last conversation this afternoon?'

'Now, Miss Knibb,' said the superintendent, 'would you mind telling me why you have been paying a pound a week to this gentleman?'

'He asked for it.'

'What did he do in exchange?'

'He wrote horrible letters, and he promised to stop if I paid him a pound a week.'

'Have you got any of the letters?'

'Yes,' said Miss Knibb.

'Can I see them?'

Miss Knibb produced the letters. The superintendent read them and then said, 'Why didn't you take these letters to the police instead of paying him a pound a week?'

'I thought there'd been enough trouble with letters already.'

'Trouble with letters? What trouble with letters?' asked the superintendent.

'The letters the vicar wrote.'

'Are you sure he wrote them?' asked the superintendent.

'He's in prison for them, so of course he did,' said Miss Knibb.

'In one of these letters that you've shown me,' said the superintendent, 'this gentleman says that he saw you go into the vicarage and implies that you typed out all the letters.'

'That's quite untrue,' said Miss Knibb.

'All the more reason for bringing it to the police. Have you ever been blackmailed before?'

'Of course not.'

'If you had nothing on your conscience I simply cannot understand why, when you're blackmailed for the first time, you don't immediately seek the assistance of the police.'

'He told me not to. The letter says so.'

'But that's what blackmailers always do,' said the superintendent. 'People are frightened to go to the police if they've done anything for which they can be blackmailed, but, if the vicar wrote all those letters, you hadn't done anything at all, had you?'

'Of course I hadn't.'

'Have you a solicitor?' said the superintendent.

'Yes,' said Miss Knibb.

'Well, I think you should get in touch with him,' said the superintendent, 'and tell him this. That you are going to be charged with sending the libellous letters in respect of which the vicar was convicted and tell your solicitor that he's very welcome to be present when you are so charged. No doubt he will advise you what to say in reply to the charge. I recommend you to say nothing more at the moment unless you wish to do so.'

Before she was charged Miss Knibb had a long conference with her solicitor and counsel, Edward Broadribb. Broadribb was an able practitioner and, after he had heard the allegations against Miss Knibb, he said this, 'Now, Miss Knibb, I want you to listen most carefully to what I am about to say. It is vital that you should do so. If you are innocent of this charge I think you will be acquitted.'

'If I'm guilty,' said Miss Knibb, 'Mr Kingsdown wasn't. But he was convicted. Presumably you'd have said the same to him.'

'Yes, I should,' said counsel, 'and I should have been wrong. Everyone is wrong from time to time. But if you're innocent, he was guilty. No one would have been wrong.'

'What about Mr Kingsdown? He said he was innocent up to the last.'

'Logically, you're quite right, Miss Knibb, but I suggest that instead of finding flaws in the language which I have used we concentrate on your innocence or guilt. I repeat that *if* you are innocent I believe that you will be found so, but if you're guilty and you plead not guilty and stick to it you may well land yourself in prison. If you're guilty you've stood by and let an innocent man go to prison, and if in addition you commit perjury and try to brazen it out, it may well be that the judge will feel bound to send you to prison if you're convicted. On the other hand, if you're guilty and make a clean breast of it at once and promise never to do such a thing again, there's a good chance of your not being sent to prison or only receiving a suspended sentence.'

'D'you think I'll be convicted?' asked Miss Knibb.

'If you're guilty, I think it very probable, but only you know that.'

'Yes, but you with your experience must have a feeling about it. Do you *think* I'm guilty?'

'Before I can answer that,' said counsel, 'will you tell me why you let a complete stranger extract a pound a week from you. Unless you can give some plausible explanation for your behaviour, I should come to the conclusion that you were guilty and so, I think, would the jury.'

'What explanation do you suggest?' asked Miss Knibb.

'It's not for me to make up explanations.'

'But you're my lawyer. Isn't that one of your jobs?'

'Certainly not. It's for me to put forward your case to the best of my ability but not to make up a case for you.'

'I bet some lawyers do.'

'Well, I don't, Miss Knibb. What is your explanation? At the moment I don't understand why a respectable woman with nothing to fear allowed a blackmailer to extract money from her without going to the police.'

'I suppose you'd think it too lame just to say that I didn't want to be mixed up with the police.'

'But when you received a poison-pen letter after Mr Kingsdown was in prison you sent that to the police. This was something far more serious. There are few things worse in life, I should imagine, than to be threatened by a blackmailer. He may bully you for the rest of your life.'

'He offered to settle for fifty pounds,' said Miss Knibb.

'But as an intelligent person you must have realised that he might not keep his word. That's a regular trick of a blackmailer. They offer to take a lump sum and promise never to come back for more. And as soon as they've spent the lump sum, they break their promise.'

'I ought to have thought of that,' said Miss Knibb, 'but quite frankly I didn't.'

'That still doesn't explain why you were prepared to pay this stranger fifty pounds, if he hadn't some hold over you.'

Miss Knibb was silent for half a minute. 'So you think I'd better admit it all?' she said. 'It will make me look such a damn fool.'

'That's better than going to prison.'

'I shall have to leave the neighbourhood.'

'No doubt. But, if you're sent to prison, you'll still have to leave the neighbourhood.'

After another half-hour's discussion Miss Knibb threw in her hand. 'All right,' she said. 'Guilty.'

'I must be quite certain of that,' said counsel. 'I don't want you to plead guilty unless you really are. Remember that I can't guarantee that you won't be sent to prison and I don't want you to say afterwards that you only pleaded guilty because you were trying to avoid being sent to prison.'

'But that's the truth, isn't it?' said Miss Knibb.

'If the truth is that you're innocent, I won't let you plead guilty.'

'I didn't say that.'

'You mean you really are guilty?'

'I've said so.'

'I know, but do you really mean it?'

'How many times do you want me to repeat it?'

'If it's the truth, I don't want you to repeat it.'

'Well, it is the truth.'

'Then why did you send the letters?'

'I was bored, I suppose,' said Miss Knibb. 'There's no excitement in Pendlebury. I thought I would make people skip about a bit and make my own life less humdrum – and theirs too. But what I can't understand is why I should have been suspected.'

Later Miss Knibb pleaded guilty, was fined £250 and given a suspended sentence of six months' imprisonment. Before she was sentenced she was asked if she wanted to say anything.

'I still can't see why I was suspected.'

That was the question Margaret asked Julian when they were discussing the matter shortly after Miss Knibb had pleaded guilty and Mr Kingsdown had been released and had his conviction quashed by the Court of Appeal.

'Why *did* you suspect her?' Margaret asked.

'Just a matter of language, really,' said Julian. 'She prevaricated when I asked her a direct question. Wholly innocent people don't.'

'It was very clever of you, darling,' said Margaret. 'You really have been enjoying your hunt for the truth. I believe you've enjoyed it more than being on the Bench.'

'It's possible,' said Julian, 'but I doubt it.'

'Your fixation for the truth has certainly been a godsend to you. I don't know what I'd have done with you if you hadn't got that to play with. But I wonder whether your reliance on mere words is always right.'

'It's not conclusive,' said Julian, 'but it's a very strong pointer.'

'I wonder,' said Margaret. 'Tell me frankly, darling, have you never told me a lie?'

'What should I want to tell you a lie for?' said Julian.

Henry Cecil

According to the Evidence

Alec Morland is on trial for murder. He has tried to remedy the ineffectiveness of the law by taking matters into his own hands. Unfortunately for him, his alleged crime was not committed in immediate defence of others or of himself. In this fascinating murder trial you will not find out until the very end just how the law will interpret his actions. Will his defence be accepted or does a different fate await him?

The Asking Price

Ronald Holbrook is a fifty-seven-year-old bachelor who has lived in the same house for twenty years. Jane Doughty, the daughter of his next-door neighbours, is seventeen. She suddenly decides she is in love with Ronald and wants to marry him. Everyone is amused at first but then events take a disturbingly sinister turn and Ronald finds himself enmeshed in a potentially tragic situation.

> 'The secret of Mr Cecil's success lies in continuing to do superbly what everyone now knows he can do well.'
> *The Sunday Times*

Henry Cecil

Brief Tales from the Bench

What does it feel like to be a Judge? Read these stories and you can almost feel you are looking at proceedings from the lofty position of the Bench.

With a collection of eccentric and amusing characters, Henry Cecil brings to life the trials in a County Court and exposes the complex and often contradictory workings of the English legal system.

'Immensely readable. His stories rely above all on one quality – an extraordinary, an arresting, a really staggering ingenuity.'
New Statesman

Brothers in Law

Roger Thursby, aged twenty-four, is called to the bar. He is young, inexperienced and his love life is complicated. He blunders his way through a succession of comic adventures including his calamitous debut at the bar.

His career takes an upward turn when he is chosen to defend the caddish Alfred Green at the Old Bailey. In this first Roger Thursby novel Henry Cecil satirizes the legal profession with his usual wit and insight.

'Uproariously funny.' *The Times*

'Full of charm and humour. I think it is the best Henry Cecil yet.' P G Wodehouse

HENRY CECIL

HUNT THE SLIPPER

Harriet and Graham have been happily married for twenty years. One day Graham fails to return home and Harriet begins to realise she has been abandoned. This feeling is strengthened when she starts to receive monthly payments from an untraceable source. After five years on her own Harriet begins to see another man and divorces Graham on the grounds of his desertion. Then one evening Harriet returns home to find Graham sitting in a chair, casually reading a book. Her initial relief turns to anger and then to fear when she realises that if Graham's story is true, she may never trust his sanity again. This complex comedy thriller will grip your attention to the very last page.

SOBER AS A JUDGE

Roger Thursby, the hero of *Brothers in Law* and *Friends at Court*, continues his career as a High Court judge. He presides over a series of unusual cases, including a professional debtor and an action about a consignment of oranges which turned to juice before delivery. There is a delightful succession of eccentric witnesses as the reader views proceedings from the Bench.

'The author's gift for brilliant characterisation makes this a book that will delight lawyers and laymen as much as did its predecessors.' *The Daily Telegraph*

OTHER TITLES BY HENRY CECIL AVAILABLE DIRECT
FROM HOUSE OF STRATUS

Quantity		£	$(US)	$(CAN)	€
	ACCORDING TO THE EVIDENCE	6.99	11.50	15.99	11.50
	ALIBI FOR A JUDGE	6.99	11.50	15.99	11.50
	THE ASKING PRICE	6.99	11.50	15.99	11.50
	BRIEF TALES FROM THE BENCH	6.99	11.50	15.99	11.50
	BROTHERS IN LAW	6.99	11.50	15.99	11.50
	THE BUTTERCUP SPELL	6.99	11.50	15.99	11.50
	CROSS PURPOSES	6.99	11.50	15.99	11.50
	DAUGHTERS IN LAW	6.99	11.50	15.99	11.50
	FATHERS IN LAW	6.99	11.50	15.99	11.50
	FRIENDS AT COURT	6.99	11.50	15.99	11.50
	FULL CIRCLE	6.99	11.50	15.99	11.50
	HUNT THE SLIPPER	6.99	11.50	15.99	11.50
	INDEPENDENT WITNESS	6.99	11.50	15.99	11.50

ALL HOUSE OF STRATUS BOOKS ARE AVAILABLE FROM GOOD BOOKSHOPS OR
DIRECT FROM THE PUBLISHER:

Internet: www.houseofstratus.com including author interviews, reviews, features.

Email: sales@houseofstratus.com please quote author, title and credit card details.

OTHER TITLES BY HENRY CECIL AVAILABLE DIRECT
FROM HOUSE OF STRATUS

Quantity		£	$(US)	$(CAN)	€
	MUCH IN EVIDENCE	6.99	11.50	15.99	11.50
	NATURAL CAUSES	6.99	11.50	15.99	11.50
	NO BAIL FOR THE JUDGE	6.99	11.50	15.99	11.50
	NO FEAR OR FAVOUR	6.99	11.50	15.99	11.50
	THE PAINSWICK LINE	6.99	11.50	15.99	11.50
	PORTRAIT OF A JUDGE	6.99	11.50	15.99	11.50
	SETTLED OUT OF COURT	6.99	11.50	15.99	11.50
	SOBER AS A JUDGE	6.99	11.50	15.99	11.50
	TELL YOU WHAT I'LL DO	6.99	11.50	15.99	11.50
	UNLAWFUL OCCASIONS	6.99	11.50	15.99	11.50
	THE WANTED MAN	6.99	11.50	15.99	11.50
	WAYS AND MEANS	6.99	11.50	15.99	11.50
	A WOMAN NAMED ANNE	6.99	11.50	15.99	11.50

ALL HOUSE OF STRATUS BOOKS ARE AVAILABLE FROM GOOD BOOKSHOPS OR
DIRECT FROM THE PUBLISHER:

Hotline: UK ONLY: **0800 169 1780**, please quote author, title and credit card
details.
INTERNATIONAL: **+44 (0) 20 7494 6400**, please quote author, title,
and credit card details.

Send to: **House of Stratus**
24c Old Burlington Street
London
W1X 1RL
UK

<u>Please allow following carriage costs per ORDER</u>
<u>(For goods up to free carriage limits shown)</u>

	£(Sterling)	$(US)	$(CAN)	€(Euros)
UK	1.95	3.20	4.29	3.00
Europe	2.95	4.99	6.49	5.00
North America	2.95	4.99	6.49	5.00
Rest of World	2.95	5.99	7.75	6.00
Free carriage for goods value over:	50	75	100	75

PLEASE SEND CHEQUE, POSTAL ORDER (STERLING ONLY), EUROCHEQUE, OR INTERNATIONAL MONEY ORDER (PLEASE CIRCLE METHOD OF PAYMENT YOU WISH TO USE) MAKE PAYABLE TO: STRATUS HOLDINGS plc

Order total including postage:_____Please tick currency you wish to use and add total amount of order:

☐ £ (Sterling)   ☐ $ (US)   ☐ $ (CAN)   ☐ € (EUROS)

VISA, MASTERCARD, SWITCH, AMEX, SOLO, JCB:

☐☐☐☐☐☐☐☐☐☐☐☐☐☐☐☐☐☐☐☐☐☐☐☐☐

Issue number (Switch only):

☐☐☐

Start Date: **Expiry Date:**

☐☐/☐☐   ☐☐/☐☐

Signature: _____

NAME: _____

ADDRESS: _____

_____

POSTCODE: _____

Please allow 28 days for delivery.

Prices subject to change without notice.
Please tick box if you do not wish to receive any additional information. ☐

House of Stratus publishes many other titles in this genre; please check our website (**www.houseofstratus.com**) for more details